SPACEACHE
SNOO WILSON

CHATTO & WINDUS · THE HOGARTH PRESS
LONDON

Published in 1984 by
Chatto & Windus · The Hogarth Press
40 William IV St, London WC2N 4DF

British Library Cataloguing in Publication Data

Wilson, Snoo
    Spaceache.
    I. Title
    823'.914[F]   PR6073.I/

    ISBN 0-7011-2785-6
    ISBN 0-7011-2786-4   Pbk

Copyright © Snoo Wilson 1984

Typeset by Rowland Phototypesetting Ltd, Bury St Edmunds
Printed in Great Britain by Redwood Burn Ltd,
Trowbridge, Wiltshire

As above, so below.

Chrissie looked out from the fortieth floor of the tower block and decided. Today was *It*. It was raining outside, and inside condensation poured down the walls of the government vertical housing. It was her birthday, Chrissie was sixteen. At sixteen, you could sign a form for the government Cryogenic Programme. They still wanted some kind of parental agreement in theory, but in effect the state had become everyone's parents. Any official, from recruiting officers through nurses to probationary jailers, could sign, on anyone's behalf, the flimsy carbon-backed Cryogenic Release Form. Cryogenesis froze the still-living bodies of volunteers and 'social deviants' and kept unemployment at a controllable figure. Chrissie had decided that she would be cryogenically frozen along with the rest of the unwanted, to await the dawning of the New Age the barest tickle of a molecule above Absolute Zero.

Chrissie tripped down the concrete stairs in her well-worn rhinestone clogs, past the urine-drenched lifts and their smashed emergency lights, over the half-burnt mattresses and their cargoes of singed prophylactics, over the mountains of broken milk bottles. This was England, and milk was still delivered in bottles. It was one of the government's election pledges, to nourish what remained of the poor. Milk carried the day, being cheap and plentiful, and the government swept into office. However the nuclear policy which was another plank in the election campaign meant that the same milk carried huge doses of strontium, such an excellent mimic of calcium that it passed into the bones of the children of the proletariat, giving them quite the wrong kind of glow.

By the time Chrissie reached the ground another thousand cryos would have been frozen. Terminal cancer patients as well as recidivists and the unemployed nearly all 'went for a Cryo', as earlier generations had 'gone for a soldier'. Right from the beginning, no Cryos were ever stored on Earth. The civil service, the permanent executive of the government of the day and sheet-anchor of a nation in desperate decline, blocked the move. An internal memo had painted a ghastly picture of what would happen if the freezers failed. There would be a mass uprising. The armies of the unemployed, the memo stated, would rise like the very nightmare of communism itself, and rend the terrified mandarins limb from limb. It was unthinkable that so many undesirables should be on earth kept at bay by mere cryogenic sleep. The memo worked, and at great expense the Cryos were now matter-reduced to three pounds and stored in high orbit round the earth.

Matter reduction was new and dangerous and very little was known about it. But every day, the big coils of the electro booster shook with a massive current and spat the cryo freighters into orbit. The coils sat on a lattice scaffolding pointing upwards, looking like an unpleasantly modern rollercoaster. There were more of them wrapped round the launching funnel which reached deep into the earth. When the rockets emerged from the funnel they were already breaking the sound barrier. It was a technological marvel, pushed through in the teeth of opposition by nature, whose objections to the programme could be heard in the shrill miaowing bellow which shook the ground and broke windows for miles around the Gatwick launchpad.

The matter-reduced Cryos were stored in chromed versions of metal milkbottles, with a reassuringly big, chunky bottle-top, computer-sealed, guaranteed not to leak under any circumstances. But the intense cold of cryo made the metal weak and brittle, and many were broken during takeoff. The opaque, syrupy fluid of matter reduction remained stable up to minus two hundred degrees, so the crew generally logged the mission as without incident, and left the satellites in orbit, knowing that no one was coming to look at them for a million years. In the orbital containers, complete strangers became mixed together beyond the hope of any centrifuge separating them out.

The pathway to the stars was not just used for curing unemployment, however. In the heavens there were also hunter satellites, killer satellites, particle-beam satellites for the comfort and protection of both sides, and satellites filled with viruses so malevolent that they could not be contained and corroded the satellite after a few years, and were then abandoned to float round and round the earth, deaf to all control.

Chrissie however was not thinking of all the hardware going wrong over her head as she waited under the rainy skies at Battersea Park for a train to take her to Gatwick. She was being carefully monitored by the station's infrared-triggered tv monitor (hooligans and drunks were hot) which kept on pointing provocatively at her navel. Chrissie bent down to make a face at it before she got on the train. Anyone could go for an interview, a Prior, for a cryo. Passes on rail and bus were free, from anywhere on the mainland.

Chrissie was dressed for the interview in a soiled white sweatshirt, silver miniskirt and the rhinestone clogs. She wore stockings with the pattern of fish scales on them. Her ex-heroine had been a mermaid, who had had a series on tv. But it was meant to be for children, and Chrissie was slightly ashamed of wanting to be something as soppy as a mermaid. Her boyfriend Ranulph had mocked her for it.

'I'm not fucking no mermaid.' He did so, regularly, but Chrissie didn't really like it. She didn't take precautions either, but this didn't seem to affect the issue one way or the other as far as he was concerned. She mentioned it in protest after one night when he'd not let her alone for a minute to drink her barley wine.

'I'm not taking any precautions,' she said, trying to look him in the eye and share this responsibility with another person. But he had turned the tables on her.

'That's all right,' he said. 'Girl, I *want* you to get fucking pregnant.'

After that, they carried on sleeping together, when she went over to his place, but both of them avoided mentioning the subject again. It was better than staying at home, Chrissie felt, but it was still not good enough. The future had to be better than *that*.

Chrissie went through the turnstiles and down into the vaults of the Gatwick Cryogenic Centre, which was built deep in the earth to escape atomic vengeance and was a circular building with eternally curved corridors, round the central funnel of the launching apparatus. She found the right office by following the worn carpet. Finally a young man appeared. His sweatshirt said I'M IN CHARGE, but Chrissie doubted if he was a real Xontroller, because he looked far more worried than Xontrollers looked on tv. Chrissie, even at her age, knew the difference between concern and worry. Concern was something that *they* expressed on behalf of the Proles. (The government's attempts to alter spelling to its own sub-Shavian standardisations had failed miserably. Proles continued to use the outlawed 'c', applications to Xryo dropped off, forcing the government to restore spelling to the people.) Xontrollers weren't Proles, they should display concern, not worry. As it turned out, Chrissie was almost right. The Xontroller, far from doing his job, seemed to be totally out of sympathy with the Cryogenic Programme.

'You know you don't get unemployment benefit if you're suspended by the central authority, *ever*? Not even in a million years. You know that they wipe you off the books?' Chrissie nodded back at him. 'And do you know also that the programme isn't safe?' This was so ridiculous that Chrissie burst out laughing. There were so many things in modern life that weren't safe that it had stopped being a yardstick of whether you did something any more.

'Apart from the initial dangers, not enough is known about the long-term effects of matter-reduction.' The Xontroller had a sample milkbottle on his desk, with an old-fashioned date seal. This was a plug of lead stamped over twisted wire, like the ones the electricity authorities used to try and stop Proles stealing power from them. And it had been a stroke of genius to make the containers like milkbottles. For what harm could ever come from a bottle of milk? The Xontroller was going on at Chrissie about how badly designed the crates for stacking the bottles were and how easily the bottles broke in subzero temperatures. But Chrissie knew that as a Prole, cryo was hers by law. It was, after all, the People's Choice, in this trying world.

'My mum and dad don't have a fallout shelter. Anyhow, we don't get on.' They both knew that these were both Adequate and Sufficient Reasons for anyone to apply for their Rights. Chrissie didn't want to leave any room for doubt, though. '*And* I don't like my boyfriend. And his family don't have a fallout shelter either.' Chrissie's boyfriend was an ignorant glucsniffing alcoholic sixteen-year-old with glue sores round his mouth and lice round his erection from his intransigent attitude to personal hygiene. The Xontroller mistook her tone for one of regret and leant forward solicitously.

'Are you upset then after breaking up with him, perhaps?' Chrissie knew that romance in this case had turned out poorly, but she didn't want the Xontroller's sympathy.

Next, the Xontroller asked her if she was pregnant. Chrissie knew that for some reason if you were pregnant they didn't let you on. Chrissie had never wanted to be pregnant, and believed it could never happen to her, especially if she was going to escape from the infested clutches of Ranulph and his hideous schemes for impregnation.

'I'm not pregnant now and I don't want to be pregnant, that's why I'm going into the future. It'll all be automated.'

The Xontroller droned on about declining safety standards, the dangers of sudden reconversion, when matter-reduced Cryos would come back into the world literally inside out. Pregnant women apparently were at even more risk, because you could exchange characteristics with the foetus. The Xontroller reached into his desk and brought out two photographs. One was of an adult, a woman. But the face was the face of a young foetus, and the 'adult' had gills, while the tiny foetus stared intelligently at the camera, a perfectly formed mature human, thirty-five years old and three inches long. The Xontroller pointed at the giant foetus photograph, and explained that she had died because her lungs were undeveloped. Chrissie noticed that his eyes were full of tears. Why on earth was he putting on this soppy show? She thought it was weird and disgusting that he should be waving photos of freaks under her nose when all she'd come for was a Prior. She wasn't going until tomorrow. What was he trying to do to her?

In the end, he put the photographs away, and asked Chrissie what she thought she was going to come back to in a million years. Chrissie shrugged.

'I'm going to leave five pounds in my savings account for when I come back. It should be worth quite a bit in a million years.'

She read the Xontroller's name off his lapel badge. It said CARWASH. That was a good Prole name. 'Come *on*. You're one of *us*, aren't you?' Carwash blushed, and shifted in his seat while his hand trembled over the Consent Form. He began to speak haltingly of the future as a con-trick and the government as illusionists as shabby as the men who ripped off the tourists in Oxford Street with 'Find the Lady', but his audience was restless.

'In the future, the shopping will be automatically delivered, and you'll be able to fuck people over the phone. When I come back, the whole world will be clean, and they'll have chucked the dirty nuclear stuff back in the sun where it belongs.' Along with most Proles, Chrissie believed that the government's monopoly of nuclear power and devices was simply an extension of the powers of the sun on earth, and that the sun was a nuclear reactor, only some considerable distance away, and could be used as a bonfire to burn man's unwanted toys. In the Future, that is. Now the only things that went into the sun were matter-reduced enemies of the state, who amidst much tv pageantry were sent into the blazing corona of the sun to reconvert.

Chrissie wondered if the Xontroller was waiting to be offered sexual favours. If he was, she wasn't going to make the first move. The Mermaid had been often put into compromising positions by corrupt police chiefs, who would mutter 'Suck on *this*', but the Xontroller, again, didn't look like one of those. He looked so worried Chrissie knew he must have a Guilty Secret but she didn't want to be around when it came out. She hoped he wasn't the one to do the medical. He looked like he was a *peep*. What a creep. In the end, however, he signed the form. The medical happened the following day, before cryogenesis.

'But can't I know now? What if I fail the medical?' Chrissie's fears of looking stupid rose up like a flock of birds. But the Xontroller reassured her.

'Don't worry. No one ever fails the medical.' Chrissie wondered why he sounded so depressed about such good news.

The doors of the train hissed shut behind Chrissie and she lit a cigarette in the empty compartment. She felt pleased. The cryo had come just in time. She had avoided all the problems of being unemployed. She would have had to go whoring to get some more fishscale tights; since the series finished you couldn't lift them from the shops any more, you had to send money away to Barnsley to get them. Her disgusting father who had molested her for the last six years would be finally put out of reach, in a way which showed him just what she thought of him. She settled back and hummed the catchy melody of the government cryo song. With its cunningly designed hook, it always brought you back at the end of the song to the beginning again:

Superprole! We treasure your hologram,
And kiss your memory lane!

NAME
CARWASH
PREVIOUS CONVICTIONS
NIL
OCCUPATION
DEPUTY SENIOR XONTROLLER, GOVT. CRYOGENICS PRO-
GRAMME
DESCRIPTION
SUSPECT IS CAUCASIAN, LIGHT BLOND HAIR, BLUE EYES,
HIGH FOREHEAD, PROMINENT CHEEKBONES. LARGE WELL
FORMED MOUTH. HEIGHT FIVE FOOT TEN. LARGE FEET,
TAPERING HANDS, SPATULATE FINGERNAILS.
PURPOSE OF REQD. INVESTIGATION
GOVT. SECURITY ACTUALISATION I-A.
SANCTIONING BODY
HAMMERSMITH ENFORCEMENT AREA
FILE ACCESS COMMAND MODE
RESTRICTED !4BA
COMPUTER ALLOCATION TIME REQUESTED
UNLIMITED
REMARKS
NO EXISTING SECURITY FILE ON SUSPECT. POSSIBLE
ALIAS CARSHAW.
STATUS OF FILE
AWAITING PROCESS BB/Q 234263546273.
RESULTS
FILE REQUEST DENIED. RECORDS SHOW CARWASH IS
CLEARED I-A
FURTHER ACTION
REPEAT REQUEST
RESPONSE
FILES FULL. QUIT AND DELETE FILE.
DELETE CARWASH#
QUIT

No-one in Surveillance could ever find out who it was in Enforcement who was looking after Carwash. It was in fact Carwash's father, now dead, who had had the computer fixed. You needed real influence to rewrite a state computer programme.

Chrissie was right to suspect that Carwash was not a true Prole. He was a rebel against The Establishment, but his father was a judge, last of a long line. Carwash, to everyone's annoyance, had succeeded in obtaining a number of rulings against individuals trying to take the Cryogenic Programme. Carwash enjoyed his position as thorn in the side of the administration, and knew many of the judges of his father's generation. His father had died recently, having been senile for some years, but it was still impossible to change the law to make judges retire. After all they *made* the law, and recently they had suddenly taken the pleas for cost-effectiveness to heart, and agreed to let justice go video. The electronic transfer of information, or *infosplosion*, was at last going to let justice pay for itself.

That was the plan, anyhow. The nightmare of paperwork, referrals, endless remand, appeals, inadmissible evidence, sleepy or bent juries, could all be resolved electronically. There was the judge, the witnesses' testimony on video with the voice of the unseen barrister asking questions, and the jury was a set of twelve Random Selection Everyman computers. The taste profiles of the Everyman were punitively democratic. Like the average man, they were in favour of capital punishment, wanted the blacks out of the country and thought that queers should be castrated; the last a trifle surprisingly since amidst much fanfare the state had programmed one and a half of the R.S.E.s to have homosexual 'tendencies'.

Carwash had been an aesthete at university, and had marched against the Nuclear Defence programme. Normally this would have meant permanent exile from jobs in the government, but such was the influence of the judges that Carwash's father had managed to create a troublefree record for his son by having him change his name slightly. The family was called Carshaw. Provided his son kept out of trouble, no-one need know.

Thus it was that Carwash, who liked to think of himself as the scourge of The Establishment, was now driving up the Thames valley, away from London, to see an old friend of his father's. Carwash had done the drive often for an appeal. Sometimes he was successful, although his success rate had dropped sharply since his father died. It was as if the judges were from their country houses, collectively telling him to pipe down. But Carwash carried on, daring them to expose him.

The judge's house had been built by a beer baron's son in the year of Jack the Ripper. When the son had come into his father's fortune he had poured his father's cellar into the river, but kept the money. Judges had become targets for animosity, and there was an electric fence, and armed guards with walkie-talkies. Carwash, however, was recognised by the butler, who let him in.

All through the journey Carwash had thought of Chrissie, how she might never know how he had risked his hide to save her, and he felt pleased. He looked out over the judge's estate. Lawns gave on to beech woods, and there was a valley thick with ripe barley, with the motorway in the distance. And was Chrissie to lose all this? Carwash had grown up in the country without paying it much attention, but now his eyes began to mist over. He imagined himself showing the view to Chrissie. Chrissie, who would barely recognise a cow and had never stepped inside a judge's house, could perhaps even become Galatea to his Pygmalion, proof to the state that the Proles were worth something.

Carwash was shown by the butler into the study where the judge gave his justice to the world. One of the results of the infosplosion that gave the judges their chance was that the powerful could always buy information and have it laid at their fingertips via a computer console. Justice was so swift now that all real and imagined crimes against the state could be dealt with immediately.

Almost everybody had a record of some sort, and the prisons were fuller than ever, making justice more expensive. Infosplosion had meant everyone was guilty of something. The judges were feared by almost everyone.

Three remote-controlled video cameras faced the judge. The studio-manager-and-usher fussed around the back hanging blue drapes over bookshelves so that later on she could mix in a different background for the judge, showing him to be sitting in a courtroom. A monitor showed the prisoner in his cell, asleep. Carwash watched in horror as two trusties walked into camera and proceeded to wake him up violently. The prisoner's face would be intercut with the judge's during the sentencing. The stusher was now fiddling with the video screen of the autojury, needlessly polishing it with a chamois leather. Finally she went into the control booth, and the judge spoke to Carwash without taking his eyes off the autojury.

'Well, Xontroller, what brings you to the judge in his chambers?' The judge had avoided the issue of his name, so far, and was pretending he didn't know why Carwash was there.

'Prole Marginals on the Cryogenics Programme.' Carwash put the form unasked for in the judge's ermine-fringed lap. The judge looked down at the flimsy paper with his shrewd blue eyes, set rather too close together, eyes that had made a small fortune out of broadcasting justice, so that it bounded from morning television to peak time. The judge was handsome too, though rather too small and thin. These things didn't show up on the tv. An exact man, he knew he had nine and half a minutes to deal with old Carshaw's son before the autojury came through. The stusher in the booth was busy editing the next week's trials – he hardly ever saw a trial in its entirety. A good stusher could edit a long trial down to a few hours. The stushers, like the judges, were paid by the speed of results, though they never got a tenth of what judges got: stushers were after all women, and should be grateful to be employed at all.

The judge looked up, having read the release form. His lips were drawn back in a smile, Carwash realised. This meant trouble.

'Don't say you've fallen for a *Praeul*.' The judge gave it its old acronymic pronunciation, only used now by official bodies and the BBC. PRAEUL stood for 'Prior to Release of Atomic Energy for Universal Liberty'. Plenty of atomic energy had been released, most of it accidentally, but Universal Liberty had been seriously in decline for some years. Carwash and the judge gazed at the monitor.

The trusties, under the guise of bringing the prisoner breakfast, were now taking it in turns to bugger him, only hampered by a shortage of prison soap. The accused was a political agitator. The judge turned the sound up so the screams could be heard faintly, and then down again. This bit would not be going on the tv. Carwash felt sick, angry and humiliated. The judge shrugged.

'Prison means nothing to these people.' The judge was about to deliver sentence on the man. The hand of the law was heavy on any kind of agitation, and electronic surveillance had increased the numbers of candidates for the ravening mill of justice. Justice pressed agitation so hard, and had its fingers so gripped round its throat, that it was difficult for agitation even to try to breathe without making justice even more cross. The judge viewed this process with amused resignation, like his own monthly tupping of the stusher. He could imagine old Carshaw's son falling for a busty snub-nosed plebeian, smelling of unwashed cunt. He was shy with women of his own class, as well: hence the necessity for an obliging stusher. Carwash had blushed at his opening joke. Obviously it had been true. Carwash had fallen for a Prole. Well well.

The judge had invented a new kind of capital punishment. Prisoners were cryogenically frozen, then dropped into the sun in a matter-reduced container. The heat as the container approached the sun's corona would burst the bottle and reconversion would occur, spilling the offender out into the wastes of space, generally inside out. His conversion, asphyxiation and carbonisation could all be watched on tv. The Feely papers had christened him 'The Burning Judge'.

The Feely papers were miracles of modern technology. On the

inside page, when you opened it, the paper became electrostatically charged, so that in the air above the paper you could recreate the 'feel' of whatever it was that had been printed on to the paper, in three dimensions. The Feely lasted for half an hour, after which it began to fade. There was not much to read in a Feely. They mostly felt. Usually they sold to the lonely; not surprisingly the Feelies consisted of men or women with their legs in the air. It was possible to make love to a Feely, if you weren't fussy. Carwash had done it once.

Carwash wanted to prove to the judge that he had the highest motives in trying to save Chrissie. He had those as well, but had also undressed her several times in his imagination, rescued her from situations worse than the one being faced by the prisoner on the monitor, and rolled with her in a deep dark bed doing exactly the same as the warders, except that this time Chrissie shouted for more.

'In this case the parents have signed the consent form with an X. They can't read.'

The judge nodded as if agreeing with Carwash. 'I'm sure the social worker will have explained it all to them. There's no chance I can stop this one. It's in a tower block, the family are D/E classification. She hasn't appealed against being sent. She wants to go. Surely it's against even your principles to come between a *Praeul* and her sincere wish? Why not let Nature take its course?'

The autojury was still deliberating with itself and the judge decided to take young Carshaw, as he thought of him, into his confidence and try to stop him doing anything foolish.

'It is far better that she does what she wants to do than she get pregnant by some petty hoodlum, and then they and their brats have to live off the state. She has sought out her own remedy. Her disease is that she's not wanted. Better not to have been born at all, in the present situation. And now, fortunately, technology has given us the means of remedying the fault.'

Carwash raised his eyebrows. The judge began to justify himself.

'Of course, it is not *entirely* her *fault* she was born a *Praeul*. The fault, dear Brutus, lies not in her, but in her stars.' The judge's wilful misquotation was not answered as expected by a smile from Carwash, although he knew *Julius Caesar* well enough. Carwash stood, unable to go, holding the death warrant of a young girl in his hand, a young girl about whom he had had, since yesterday, numerous desperate fantasies. Carwash's heart filled with black hatred of the judge, his father, and the whole of the civil service and ruling class, the armed forces, royalty and the clergy. He mentally erased his ties with his background and put himself with a rifle on the barricades made out of police computers, with Chrissie at his side.

The judge meanwhile was talking amiably about the influence of planets on Shakespeare's characters, and how easy it was in those days to accept the paradoxes of determinism in astrology, since they had no way of finding out if the outer planets were there at all. The judge had always ridden a little hobbyhorse about astrology, and fancied he could guess prisoners' sun signs, and had even suggested that malefic transits could trigger crimes against the state. Suddenly however his tone changed and he was talking about Carwash again.

'Not that *astrology* means anything to you people on the *ultra-left*.' The judge, when giving judgement, always stressed words of definition. That way Proles knew that it was his definition, or rather the state's. When the judge said 'astrology' in private, it meant something he was interested in. When he sat in judgement and said '*astrology*', a host of ghostly fakers, buskers and influence-mongers were included in his scornfully directed tone. This was the tone he had used with Carwash, who jumped, though he didn't know what he was going to be accused of. Then he remembered.

He had abandoned the Left, long ago, when he changed his name and got a job. But recently, he'd met some of his old friends from the university, who'd gone underground after they'd mounted a campaign against cryogenic suspension.

They'd met in a pub and Carwash had given them some money and left in a hurry, afraid that his own disguise might be discovered. Now he knew that the group were being watched. Which meant that he was being watched too. It was useless to deny anything. Much better to be like the Proles, forget, obliterate, become ignorant, so that the cruellest lie-detector could not grub the truth out of you.

'I'm afraid I don't know what you're talking about,' Carwash said.

The judge put his skinny arm round Carwash and walked him to the study door. He had two and a half minutes to go. At the door of the house, he bent with his stooped back to pick the electronic mail off the printer which hung on the back of the door. His back was thin and rose to his spine from both sides in a repellent sharp arch. Carwash wondered if he should take one of the ornamental stone lions and smash the old man to a pulp. They'd torch him for that for sure, the Boy Who Killed The Burning Judge. The Proles would know why though, know that really he was one of them:

> Superprole! We treasure your hologram,
> And kiss your memory lane!

But he wasn't brave enough yet for what Chrissie was doing; self-immolation. He wasn't brave at all, he thought, as the judge passed before him into the afternoon sun. The security system beeped politely, but the judge left the door open. There was something else he wanted to say.

'Many, many people of moral integrity who begin by opposing the state end by supporting it. What else is there?' Carwash thought, *Good. They haven't caught me yet. That means I'm still free, and free means free to act.* But the judge continued, looking absurdly cranky in his huge robes standing outside in the sunlight, squinting up at Carwash.

'This is the gypsy's warning. You cannot continue to hold your present job, and meet opponents of the Cryogenic Programme. You may not have given them state secrets, *yet.* But if the Luddites or the right-to-life fanatics start up again, they'll catch them, and then they'll want to know why you, who were so close to them, didn't warn the state. Tell me, what are they going to do? Are they going to attack a cryogenic plant?' The old man's voice was sweet as honey and he leant in a friendly way on Carwash's arm. 'Because, if they do, they will be *murderers*, and punished as such by being sent on *Solar Impact Orbit*.' Carwash wanted to drive off but the old man wouldn't take his head out of the car window. He had bad teeth and bad breath, but he was warming to an official theme, while checking his watch to see that he could still be in the studio on time. Already he was the Burning Judge, next to Carwash's face, inside his defences, paternal, threatening, confidential, kindly, *close*. 'Tell your friends, "Be you never –" ' Carwash couldn't stand it any more and began to drive off, but the old man kept pace with the car. ' "– be you never so *solar*, the law is above you." Tell them, "Put down your murdering eyes!" ' The people Carwash had met had been in the Solar Party, who refused to pay tax on energy gathered from the sun.

Carwash drove off and the judge picked up his robes and skipped back to his study with the speed of a seventy-five-year-old who hadn't gained a pound since he played squash for Oxford, and had played since every day.

The Solar Party had done well at the outset when they had restricted their demands to the abolition of nuclear weapons and nuclear energy. But later on they had become more extreme as none of their demands had been met and popular support ebbed away. The judges gave show trials of the more anarchic members who did not see why the government, who had done nothing to deserve it, should control gas, oil, wood, foodstuffs or anything else that directly or indirectly came from the sun. There were plenty of crazies who were prepared to step into the limelight under the Solar banner. It was however the Burning Judge who dreamed up the idea of putting criminals into the sun, the 'People's nuclear reactor' as the Solar Party had called it with touching inaccuracy, since the sun was a fission-fusion reaction.

Carwash drove out through the electrified fence in the mellow September sunlight and the judge sat down bright as a button to face his three video cameras. The stusher was doing the announcements over the Sleepiwake Pharmaceuticals logo (Sleepiwake, a concept you can *trust*), telling the audience that William Bunce had been found guilty of breaching state security and, friends at home, you are invited to join us for the moment of judgement.

Bunce had been thoroughly and inventively woken up by the trusties and now stood staring dumbly up at the monitor like a dying calf, another ten milligrams of quaalude coursing through his veins as a precaution against a violent reaction when the orange light went on in his cell, signalling the death sentence, like the old black cap. The judge had taken the precaution of buying Sleepiwake shares before the concept campaign had started on his station, and had seen his little nest-egg grow. He nourished the judgements with fine public presence, and a rich authority. He wrote his own scripts and could gauge the public taste as well as any actor-manager of the old days. Like them, he was playing in his own theatre; he owned the tv station and could speak for two and a half minutes, which was the attention span of a Prole, better than any of the other judges. Recently he had had his robe stitched with little astrological signs in cloth-of-gold round the collar, and had been pleased with the response. The stusher finished, Bunce yawned, and the judge was suddenly on camera, and in front rooms everywhere in the land. High in a tower block in Battersea, Chrissie was watching too.

'Citizens and Praeuletariat, good evening. *Bunce*.' Bunce had been a machinist in South London. Bunce was half West Indian. Bunce was a Moslem, who was also allergic to household dust. Bunce pulled his trousers up slowly and tried to wave to his mother, but he wasn't used to tranquillisers and the arm only made it halfway up before dropping again, what the Feelies would call BUNCE'S DEFIANT ANARCHIST SALUTE.

'Bunce took it upon himself to worm his way into the affections of a *young Government Wordprocessor*, with the sole object of obtaining *Classified Information*. Bunce, some might say a *communist*, used his vile seductions as a *cloak of darkness*, under which he thought he could penetrate to our most *vital state secrets*.' The judge had cleverly combined the idea of dirty old men and a virginal state (represented by the secretary Bunce had slept with) to produce a compelling picture of degradation. Sleepiwake climbed a point as the nation got Bunce's score card, which was that he had failed.

'Fortunately, he was stopped and the nation is still *intact*. Bunce had no privy information when he chose to resist Enforcement officers in an enquiry and, he claims accidentally, *killed* one of them.' The Enforcement ran brothels and drug rings and drove around in convoys with headlights on, horns blaring. They beat up suspects, sometimes to death. Bunce had been defending himself against their enquiries. It was not the safest of positions.

'Bunce, normal cryogenic suspension, welcomed by so many of our unfortunates and social misfits, does not seem to have posed any threat to you in your vile course.' It was true. Bunce had wanted to live. He was also against the state's unending theft of bread from the mouths of the Third World by the sale of nuclear weapons to the governments of the same Third World. Bunce had come up with the radical notion that the constant threat of nuclear annihilation was a lie. The destructive powers unleashed would be so great as to annihilate almost everything. Everybody, Bunce argued, was agreed on the fact that there was no such thing as a limited-strike nuclear war. Furthermore, he added, there would never be any other kind. Any government who was rash enough to partake in the destruction would be lynched in their shelters, *and they knew it*. It was the last phrase that particularly upset the prosecution and turned a simple execution into a televised state torching.

'Bunce, your political allegiance has led you to a position where in order to maintain law and order, I have no alternative but to provide you with a close encounter with a nuclear experience. I only hope it proves more of a deterrent to your kind than it has done in the past.'

Commuters stared in dull fascination at the giant uneven picture of the judge on the big screen at Victoria Station, then turned with their bowed heads and umbrellas and joined their trains. Over the river in Battersea, Chrissie wandered back into the room, having made herself a cup of tea. The volume was raised slightly, almost to the level of the commercials, for the judge's summary.

'Bunce, I sentence you to be taken from here and cryogenically frozen while still living. You will then be matter-reduced and kept at low temperature. You will then be placed in one of Her Majesty's Freighters, which will take you outside the gravitational field of the earth, to release you in an impact orbit with the sun, so that as your approach quickens towards its great mass, the canister containing you will heat, and at a given moment your life will reignite, bursting out of its unnatural suspension for a moment of consciousness, to the brief sketch of a man, before vaporising in the solar wind, as you fall in the glare of the great atomic furnace.'

Chrissie leant on the door frame of the tiny kitchen and

hummed as Sleepiwake's theme tune came up over the final, solemn words of the judge: 'Take the prisoner down.'

Bunce, who had never been up in the courtroom in the first place, stared dully at the orange light in his cell. It went on. Suddenly the door opened and four men in asbestos suits came in with a long hosepipe. They wore breathing masks and goggles. The hose contained liquid nitrogen. They wrapped Bunce in a prison blanket and sprayed him to freezing point in twenty seconds. In a minute he was frozen solid, and they picked him up and ran with him, stiff as a board, to the matter-reduction plant. It was quicker and more wasteful than the right method of freezing, but no-one ever asked questions any more about how much gas was needed.

Carwash saw it on the news later that night. The judge was surrounded by all the paraphernalia of the courtroom, which had been cunningly grafted in around him in his study by the stusher. Carwash saw that the fight to save Chrissie had been lost from the start. He knew his next step was to wreck a cryogenic plant. He might not do it before Chrissie got into orbit, but at least he would have shown people where he stood. And it might even sow a seed of revolt somewhere. As the Cryo Quartet used to warble softly, trying to raise the number of female Prole volunteers for the programme:

> *Throw your Wonderloaf on the water, heroine!*
> *See it return after many days!*
> *Example to the unemployed millions*
> *Voyager to post-industrial pavilions*
> *When the state shall wither away!*

Carwash decided to be a hero, if Chrissie was dumb enough to want to be a heroine. Then he felt frightened. He hadn't ever done anything like that before.

Sirens howling, an Enforcement escort had taken Bunce's frozen body from Brixton to the nearest cryo plant. Then a helicopter had sped the tiny bottle in a cooling jacket to Gatwick, and with a nausea-inducing, shrieking *whoomph* a squat government freighter had climbed laboriously through the stratosphere, with a dodgy hydraulic system, and now was parked in orbit round the sun, while the crew hand-cranked the freighter doors open to float the morsel of humanity towards the sun, which the painter Turner had said was God.

Chrissie was hungry. She scraped the mould off some jam and mixed it in with a tin of baked beans, and sat down to watch the live coverage of the execution. Nothing very much seemed to be happening because the freighter crew were still getting the doors open. There were two commentators who poured words in endless, contrapuntal streams to fill the tedious gaps in the spectacle. Chrissie watched it not without interest. Tomorrow she would be up there amongst the stars.

I think I can see movement, yes the freighter doors are opening on the sunward side. And there goes the capsule. Not making its impact trajectory as quickly as we'd hoped . . . No! There it goes, it's painted matt black for maximum heat absorption, with two orange crosses, to help friends at home pick it out against the velvet background of stars . . .

Another voice took up the thread of the commentary. They'd been on the job since the freighter took off four hours ago and were running out of happy descriptive phrases. But a job was a job and they kept on, sounding excited for other people's benefit. They were professionals.

It's traversing now in front of the constellation of Cassiopeia, moving now more quickly towards the sun. Or, it seems like that rather, because we are in fact drawing away now. It's being tracked by quite a number of radio antennae as well. Why is that, John?

Well, Martin, one of the curiosities of reconverting quickly out of matter-reduction is that there are a large number of waves – X-rays, gamma rays, radio waves, they're all produced, and it may seem heartless but it's an excellent place to study this reaction, here in space . . .

Bunce was not just a casual fly who was having his wings pulled off before being burned by the state: he had gone beyond that into the status of Scientific Experiment. There was a brief pause and Chrissie could hear the static and trilling of the radio noises of space. But the capsule remained stubbornly intact as it inched its way towards the sun.

At school, to the constant delight of her teachers, Chrissie had learned to read and write and had been bright and active. She had run and laughed and sung. Her lithe young body had a remarkably low accumulation of carcinogens, as if she almost *wanted* to live. Her mother, catching sight of her aged ten combing her mousy brown hair in the mirror, was moved to tears and wept in great shuddering jerks while she held Chrissie too tight. Chrissie had previously only thought her mother capable of showing fatigue, and the new emotion caught her by surprise, and she had hugged her mother back.

Shortly after that, her father, having taken his pension early because of his decayed lungs, what the union called 'The Asbestos Handshake', found time heavy on his hands, and with the fires of death well stoked in his chest made that an excuse to constrain Chrissie to lie with him.

Chrissie's body was starting to sprout other hair, darker than mouse. Her periods began, then ceased. She became withdrawn. At school she was a falling star in a firmament of losers. Her absolute backwardness became remarkable and her mother dragged her off to the doctor to find out why she wasn't eating and why her periods had stopped, God forbid the little girl's pregnant. Chrissie was in fact inching her way towards anorexia – the only way out of puberty short of suicide – but the doctor simply put her on the pill. Chrissie survived and her breasts enlarged so she threw the pills away. Her father's illness worsened and she became a subtle student of his moods, always managing to be away when the flame burned high. Whether she stayed at home or away, she always felt guilty. Her family, all through this time, had the feeling of unravelling under the strain, like a badly made wicker basket, and by the time she was fourteen Chrissie had already made her decision to opt for Space. (The day before her birthday Chrissie had seen the writing on the wall of the school khazi: CHRISSIS DAD GOES UP HER XUNT. It had been the final straw. She'd told one girl and that girl had told the school. Superprole! We treasure your hologram, and kiss your memory lane!)

Chrissie had gone home and told her father she was going for a Cryo the next day. He hadn't given her real trouble for some time but continued his lame requests for sexual excursions with his daughter. But Chrissie had got a boyfriend, so that sort of thing had to stop now. That was the main point of having Ranulph, after all. Her father was slowly dying as his lungs turned to spongy tissue unable to absorb oxygen. In defiance of all medical instruction he continued to smoke. His doctor knew he was dying, attributed it privately to the factory as much as the cigarettes, but all he could do was to give him nicotine chewing-gum, which got stuck in his dentures so he carried on smoking.

He came in from the kitchen where he'd lit a Woodbine off the stove and peered at the television. He looked old but he was in fact forty-five. He wore a vest and trousers which were unbuttoned. His breathing was so strenuous that he could not bear to have any pressure on his stomach. He pointed at the tv.

'All right, so what's *he* done?' Chrissie had no idea what Bunce's crime was. The telecast had been going on too long.

Chrissie's father was a folk repository of horror stories about things which went wrong with Progress, and in particular the Cryogenic Programme which he had just learnt his daughter was to embark on. Most of the stories were inaccurate in detail but alarmingly precise about its real intentions and actions. Chrissie's father was an expert on others' misfortune. He sucked as hard as he could on his Woodie, and began to hold forth on the evils of cryo.

'I bet they don't bother to freight half of them up. They say you can see sausagemeat vans backin' up to the cryogenic plants at night. Believe me, you're throwing yourself away. On a butcher.'

He made a gesture of throwing and his hand ended up on Chrissie's leg. Since the monstrous growth in his lungs had begun to blossom Chrissie had nearly always resisted him successfully. He didn't have the strength to beat her now she was bigger. He would spend hours in a daze in front of the tv, with all the lights off and his trousers unbuttoned. Chrissie moved down the sofa.

'Where's Mum?' Chrissie's mum cleaned New Scotland Yard after the Filth went home. She caught the night bus in and out. She was called Petal. Recently she had started disapproving of Chrissie's clothes and her boyfriend. Petal wore corsets and made her husband sleep in the spare room. Sexual disappointment ran in the family.

'She's working.' Chrissie's father listened in complete contempt to John and Martin who were working themselves into a lather over an almost invisible capsule. Then he said, 'Don't you want to give your old dad a good time before you pop off?'

Chrissie ignored him, for very soon Ranulph would be there. The father, not strong enough to do anything else, began to whine, despicably, and say things weren't like this in the *good* old days, when his little Chrissie used to let him have a fair crack of the whip. But Chrissie was saved from having to defend herself against an enfeebled attempt at continued abuse. Ranulph appeared behind the sofa in the light from the tv like a messenger from the gods, dressed in skin-tight leather and dark glasses. Chrissie's father began to shrink away from her immediately.

'What's he been doing then?' Ranulph was always abrupt. Her father was frightened of him. The leather boys always liked to kill someone else if they didn't manage to kill themselves before they were twenty. Chrissie was peeved with her disgusting old man and thought she'd let Ranulph teach him a lesson he'd remember after she had gone.

'He's at it again. He's always trying to get a poke. Leave *off*!' she shouted at her father, who couldn't have looked more inoffensive and meek now that Ranulph was there. Ranulph turned to the prematurely old man and wittily overacted his astonishment.

'I don't *believe* it! I'm going to have to teach him a *lesson*.' Ranulph had been seldom to school and the expression appealed to him. Chrissie's father began to cough and go purple in the face. Ranulph spoke softly to Chrissie as the old man went into spasm.

'Why don't you stop this idea of going for a Cryo? Eh?' Chrissie didn't want Ranulph to stop her, and yet the knowledge that he could stop her by beating her up till her eyes closed and the blood ran down her face and she went to the hospital rather than the cryo plant made them both a little excited and afraid, as they felt for a moment the terrible potential of love. But Chrissie wanted to freeze, not burn in love, and looked away. Ranulph picked up a bottle. The bottle was used by Chrissie's father to relieve himself in to save the long, oxygen-draining shuffle to the kitchen sink and back. The bottle was a long-standing feature of the living room but Ranulph pretended not to know anything about it. Then he playfully poured some of the liquid in it over the father's head. Chrissie was annoyed now Ranulph had started on her father, and wanted him to stop. She told him to leave off, unavailingly, then tried to cool the situation by removing her attention and pretending to watch the immolation on the tv. By this time, however, the situation with Ranulph and her father had escalated, and her father rightly feared for his life.

'Don't you dare lay a finger on me,' he said to Ranulph. Ranulph, seeing him cowering on the sofa, his face gleaming with his own urine, sick, malevolent, incestuous, decided that the moment had come to act. Chrissie's father had become an open insult to youth, beauty, and man's natural nobility, and so wide was the gap between them that Ranulph decided that the old man was no longer properly human. He decided to prove himself and strike a blow for decency all in one fell swoop, and began to beat Chrissie's father up. First he hit him about the head with the bottle, and then when the bottle wouldn't break on the old man's skull or arms, he pulled him off the sofa.

Then he kicked him in the crutch with his motorcycling boots. The father behaved according to Ranulph's idea of how he should.

He whined. He begged for mercy. Ranulph smashed him in the kidneys till his fist hurt. Then he broke the bottle on the edge of the tv, making the picture jump, and started scientifically to explore Chrissie's father with the intention of letting some blood. When he had opened him up in a few places, the flow of the father's precious, inadequately oxygenated fluid on to the floor gave Ranulph his second wind.

He pummelled and pumped. He drew up the old man's dressing-gown and started to whip his back with his studded leather belt. Chrissie told him to leave off a few times. Things had gone too far. But then she quelled her uneasiness with the thought that tomorrow she was leaving this unpleasant civilisation for something infinitely more delightful, and she just watched the tv and let them get on with it.

They were showing the capsule bursting, a smudgy blur which quickly began to glow, then disappeared. For all the judge's hoopla, the death was fairly unremarkable. The flat below started banging on the ceiling to tell them to stop the thumping. Ranulph stopped and threw himself down on the sofa next to Chrissie, saying he was whacked.

Then he started talking, more relaxed than she'd known him in a long time, as if a spring inside had been allowed to unwind. He said how disappointed he was that she hadn't been pregnant, and how he wished that she'd got one going, how he wouldn't stand in her way or anything if she really wanted to go for a Cryo – in fact he might join her in a few days – but he did, oh, he did want one last try for a baby for them both. Chrissie's heart sank at the thought of Ranulph turning up in paradise, and tried to explain to the foul-smelling, murderous lout what the problem was.

'They don't take you if you're pregnant. Understand?'

Ranulph nodded as if he understood. 'But that's it, Chrissie, you don't *get* pregnant.' There was no denying that he'd tried.

'I don't get pregnant because I don't want one.'

'I've got other girls pregnant that didn't want. It's not want that says so.' Ranulph started laboriously to peel down his leather trousers, sticky with the sweat of victory over Chrissie's dad. 'I tell you what, girl. We'll have one last run up the slope.'

Chrissie thought of the medical next morning and shook her head.

'Come on, girl, a quick wiggle.' Ranulph got up and shuffled over to the old man, pulling the carpet securely round his head so that he couldn't see. 'I'll just cover the parrot up, anyhow.' The old man's eyes had closed to puffy slits, so even if he'd been conscious he could hardly have seen a thing.

'My mum's coming back in a minute. I'm not taking my clothes off.' Ranulph cracked an amyl nitrate single-handed into his cupped hand and breathed it in, looking surprised. He pulled Chrissie's tights down so roughly that they tore, raised her reluctant legs in the air, and entered her. Chrissie was angry but the rules said you couldn't stop a man in a rush, not after what he'd done to her dad. Besides, soon she would be free of all this and it meant nothing to her, not if she didn't get pregnant. Chrissie lay quiet, not doing anything, hoping it would soon all be over. She refused the popper which Ranulph offered her. He took two. She turned her head to watch the tv.

Suddenly he was getting dressed and leaving. John was saying to Martin that it was a little disappointing visually, hardly the event that they'd hoped for.

What are you doing? Chrissie had asked Ranulph as he ruined her last pair of mermaid tights. Ranulph had hurt her as he went in. *I'm fucking you, aren't I?* he had replied when he'd got comfortable. And then he'd come.

'What are you getting up for?' Ranulph, conscious of the absurdly brief time which had elapsed, shook his shoulders well into his jacket and walked to the door before replying, 'I'm off. I've done.'

On the tv, the canister spurted and died in endless computer-processed replays as they showed Bunce's last moment of being as a whole person, albeit inside out. The fireworks which should have happened to Bunce's earthly body were a flop. Somewhere in matter-reduction, exciting nitrates had shifted to dull stable nitrides, free oxygen had moored itself to hydrogen and become mere water. Bunce had spluttered his life away. And still the state did not feel safe.

When Chrissie got herself straightened out she rang the Enforcement, and showed them her cryo card, which guaranteed her freedom from prosecution. She wouldn't have bothered, but the old man's blood had dripped through the ceiling to the flat below. She gave a video statement about Ranulph for the trial, describing him and how he had killed her father and raped her.

Then the reporters came. Chrissie didn't want to face her mother after what had happened so she was photographed at Victoria Station under the big tv screen. She was waiting to go to Gatwick on the first train at five.

The reporters left her to catch the Feely deadlines and she kept walking to avoid the crazy derelicts with anti-cryo placards, who wanted her not to go. The big screen kept running cigarette and drink advertisements in between the sweet, close-harmony cryo concept songs. Proles slept badly and left their tvs on all night. There was no doubt that it worked in the end on their strong instincts for self-preservation.

> *Going somewhere you haven't been?*
> *Come on everybody look at the queen of heaven,*
> *Heaven!*
> *The stars in her veil, and on her brow*
> *Sweet serenity makes its invisible mark now*
> *Right now!*

(The future will be all right if you fight that good fight,
The future will be fine if you shine that light!
Say one thing for the future, it is out of sight!)

Don't let's get too parvenue,
Let's reach out for something new,
A glittering pile of brand new days
For me
And you!

After the glamour of posing for forty motordriven Nikons, with strobe-like flash guns that would have given anyone less used to disco lighting than Chrissie a fit, Gatwick Cryogenic seemed less like an invitation to a life of leisure and permanent orgasm than before, especially at quarter to seven on a wet morning. The concrete was piled lavishly in massive curves above the ground, but it was streaked with stains, and stalactites had appeared where the huge complex dripped. Chrissie, in her haste to avoid further do-gooders with placards, had been forced to choose a different entrance and felt as if she was walking under a giant crab which might at any moment let its legs down and squash her with its mighty body. She pressed on.

She never found the place she had been before, though the corridors were just as endless. She was beginning to be tired, and could swear she had passed the same solitary cleaning woman a dozen times. Chrissie's mother had cleaned all her life, but Chrissie knew that there had to be more to life than cleaning in the future, or, as the advertisements put it, *The Future!*

Up until the beginning of the twentieth century, homesteaders had been able to peg out land and call it their own. But now there was nowhere for the Proles to go after the infosplosion, except the more dubious frontier of a cryogenic limbo. There were many people who found life so unbearable that they took the thin chance that cryo offered as preferable to staying on the earth, and not all of them were Proles. Bunce's belief that the nuclear defence programme was something which would never be used, because no government could govern after they had destroyed the earth, was comforting. If, however, the suicides, murders, and manslaughters were counted up with the Cryo Programme, the idea that Man was an animal whose natural bent was self-preservation began to look rather shaky.

The government breathed the same air as the self-slaughterers. Bunce was noble, Bunce was wrong, and the self-culling continued under the ambiguous shadow of nuclear 'protection'. As above, so below.

The doctors who administered the Cryogenic Programme's final inspection quickly learned that their purpose was simply a display of professional, white-coated windowdressing for the new oblivion. Like any bad habit, the programme once started was difficult to phase out, but it seemed, fortunately for the government, that space could act almost indefinitely as a dumping ground for the unwanted Proles. The Cryo Programme became the new first step into the nation's health programme for ambitious but underqualified doctors. The Indian and Pakistani medics had a long history of survival under incompetent British administration and an instinctive feel for bureaucracy. They understood that the hypocrisy of their position was the price they paid for admission to the professions in England. The doctors appeared to look after cryo so that cryo could look after the doctors.

Chrissie didn't mind Paki doctors, quite liked dark boys in general, to Ranulph's disgust. But the one facing her in the examination cubicle had an arm missing. The white sleeve of his coat was folded and pinned neatly in front like a campaign medal while from a slit in the shoulder there poured a tumble of brightly coloured wires which disappeared under the lid of a large instrument steriliser. It was dark in the cubicle but when Chrissie turned the light on he cried out in pain, shielding his eyes, which were already protected by thick bottle-green glasses with side wings. The doctor put on a special dim pink light on his desk and there was a splashing from the steriliser unit.

Many people waited up to seven years for clones when they had lost an arm or a leg. The surgeons would often give a patient an intermediate hand, usually from a laboratory rhesus monkey, so that the patient could continue to exercise the organ, squeezing a rubber ball or writing with it once a day till they reached the head of the queue for clones. But this doctor appeared to be wired to some kind of fish. He got up and turned the overhead light off again.

Now Chrissie couldn't see anything outside the pool of pink light. There was more splashing as the doctor sat down.

'What's that in the water?'

'It's my hand,' said the doctor, in a tired voice.

'But what is it *really?*' Chrissie asked anxiously. She didn't want to be examined by a lobster. The top of the steriliser unit lifted briefly to show a mass of writhing tentacles with suckers on. It was now Chrissie's turn to scream.

'It's quite all right,' the doctor said. 'It was an octopus, but it no longer obeys its brain. It's my hand.' Chrissie almost fainted at the thought of a squid examining her.

'Can't you lock the box?' The doctor shook his head and pointed to the couch, and told her to take off her dress and lie with her feet in the stirrups. The cubicle was tiny and the vinyl-covered couch was hard up against the steriliser unit. Half of it was in the dark. Chrissie didn't like the way things were turning out at all. The doctor's bottle-green glasses swept the darkness sightlessly and his stethoscope made a faint grating noise on the bare office table in front of him. Hoping to impress the doctor with her status and perhaps even skip the medical, Chrissie got out the Feely paper; she had seen herself on the cover where the visuals were. She was at Victoria Station, showing a lot of leg and looking blank. The headline said, FIEND TORTURES GYMSLIP CRYO'S DAD. She put it down on the desk, as a barrier between them. There was a brisk, cold draught blowing down the corridor from the nitrogen tanks and the paper fluttered, threatening to open up the centrespread. The cubicle was hardly big enough for the two of them and there was no way of reversing it once you had peeled open a Feely. The paper flapped again but the doctor continued to stare straight ahead.

'I'm afraid I don't touch the Feely papers,' he said. 'I find it rather distasteful that a news medium has to boost sales by encoding Feelies of complete strangers with their legs in the air.' The chill wind rustled the pages again and, horror of horrors, blew the paper open at the Feely page, which was meant to be glued shut against accidents. The paper wrinkled flatly on the desk as if pressed down by the weight of the Feely's body. But it was only static. The stethoscope of the doctor crackled as it moved across the surface. Marks like date stamps stood incomprehensibly all over the paper but Feelies were not for the eyes.

The doctor stood up. He would have to climb over the Feely to get to the couch. But he wasn't going to. He pressed his stethoscope against the Feely, moving it around sightlessly till he found its chest.

'Deep breath now,' he said. Chrissie suddenly realised that she was in luck. The blind doctor thought he was examining her when he was in fact touching a Feely, which was in the usual position on its back with its legs in the air. Chrissie could see the Feely's position from the way the doctor's hand caressed the empty air. He had a beautiful hand, with long slim fingers and slightly corrugated, hyperthyroid nails. His pinky, the messenger of Mercury, had a slight crook in it. It was absurd that he had accepted the Feely on his desk but Chrissie knew a lot of doctors who were nearly always out of it on their own drugs. The hand went further up in the air, caressing the thighs, the knees, the ankles, the feet, then back again.

'We're going to do a short internal examination.' The doctor was breathing heavily through his nose, and the octopus had started to push the lid off the steriliser. The doctor switched on a glass examining-rod with a light in it, and began thoughtfully to probe the air in front of him.

'If you experience any tenderness in the vaginal area, tell me and I'll use some cream. Tell me, have you engaged in sexual intercourse recently?' The doctor was probing the pudenda of the Feely with three fingers. Soon he would put his hand completely through the sensation shell and it would feel nothing and the illusion would collapse. The illuminated glass rod rolled off the table and fell on the floor where it continued to shine, showing row on row of dusty cryo containers under the desk. The chill wind continued to blow.

'Is the freezer down the corridor?' Chrissie asked. She could nick a bottle and walk down with it while he was still busy with the Feely. The cooling fans clattered and roared distantly. The doctor nodded. Chrissie held her breath and crept round the other side of the desk to get a bottle, when she saw something which froze her in her tracks.

The octopus had got out of the water, and was shinning its way down the doctor's leg to rescue the torch. But the wire had got caught somewhere and it couldn't quite reach. Chrissie decided to risk it and reached out and took a bottle. There was the smallest of clinks, and the octopus turned and *gave her a look*. Chrissie turned back with the bottle and stood up. The cooling fans and the squeak and chuckle of boiling nitrogen suddenly got louder as someone opened a door along the corridor. The doctor put his right hand into the Feely and it came to rest on the table. There was a brief crackle from his fingertips and the Feely shorted out and ceased to be. The doctor writhed and removed his hand. Chrissie pulled the limp Feely paper off and threw it down on the couch where it flapped softly in the wind, the static leached away. The octopus was back in its cabinet. The doctor took out a pink form, signed it and pushed it across the table to Chrissie.

'Take a container from under the table, please, and go to the third door on your right.' So the doctor had done his bit, and wasn't going to stop her going. The form alleged that her uterus was firm, pink and moist. Chrissie wasn't going to argue with that. The doctor asked if she wanted some tranquillisers.

'What would I need those for?' The doctor gave her some to take later on if she felt at all nervous. Chrissie went off to the cooler bravely, confident that she would make a better go of it in a million years. The great constellations of the zodiac would have swung round forty times by then, and things would have had to change for the better. The common fear of Cryos, that they might end up in a zoo run by more evolved creatures, or be shunted by the cargoload to make fertiliser for the asteroid belt, never crossed her mind. She threw the pills down outside the door as if she was in a drug bust at a disco. Chrissie was certain that in the end the

Proles would be victorious, and she trod lightly towards the sounds of bubbling nitrogen.

Throw your Wonderloaf on the water, heroine!
See it return after many days!

Take a ticket to ride on that ice-cold train,
Ice-cold train!
Don't overdose on sleepers, enchantress!
Death plays finders keepers, enchantress,
In his wideawake, Dayglo, customised hearse.
Walk away before it all gets worse
Walk away before it all gets worse
To the cryogenic bosom of the universe!
(Balls to Abraham!)
The universe, the cryogenic bosom of the universe!
(Bugger Abraham!)
The universe, the cryogenic bosom of the universe!
(Balls to Abraham!)
The universe,
(Etc & fade)

Chrissie lay in the cooling tank and no longer felt her body. In addition to the nitrogen there was a simultaneous electronic cooling which worked like a microwave oven in reverse, and her brain began to chill then freeze before the oxygen was cut off. Her neural synapses slowed down then stopped, and her thoughts lay like freight trains, indefinitely halted in sidings. Chrissie's body was put on a conveyor belt. She was now at minus two hundred degrees and her heart had stopped long ago. The conveyor belt jammed briefly as it often did on the way to the matter-reduction plant. The cold made the rollers stiff. An engineer slowly crawled under the belt to fix it. Chrissie had stopped opposite the door he'd accidentally left open, and framed in the door was a field of wheat being patiently reaped by a big combine harvester. The warm air blew in and a thought was released in Chrissie's brain.

Chrissie's consciousness had shrunk to a small circle of being, which contained all of her past and all of her future. She could do nothing about any of it, and was content to see herself in this way until a warm breeze laden with pollen-like chaff rustled her frosted hair, raising the temperature till she could think rather than just be. Chrissie was annoyed because she was enjoying just being, with one foot in eternity. She felt she was the centre of everything that moved, the unmoved mover of the universe, serenely acquiescent. The conveyor belt started again, but the breeze had caused the synapse to discharge its message into the circle of her untroubled consciousness.

There was nothing she could do about anything now, but she realised that the hideous Ranulph's last embrace had left an imprint on her teenage body, and that she was now, irrevocably, pregnant. The serpent had struck home at last and Chrissie wanted to scream. The Buddhists hold that the first noble truth is that all is sorrow. But Chrissie's access to this wisdom was marred in the beginning by an ugly, hysterical, impotent horror at what she might become.

Chrissie's final thought was that if that really *was* the case, then she never, ever wanted to come out. If she had anything to do with it, rather than risk coming back as a foetus with gills, she'd stay in cryo *for good*.

Naked, illicitly clutching her torn mermaid tights which she'd taken along for good luck, furious with her own bad luck, Chrissie went into matter-reduction.

Returned Cryogenics under hypnosis had reported consciousness. Doctors had dismissed the claim, pointing to the absence of brain activity. When the reading was taken with an encephalograph from the frozen brain, there were no waves on its electronic horizon. Chrissie was conscious of something, but it was more like a mood than a thought. Her mood grew and fed upon years of undischarged frustration and anger, culminating in *this*. It was like being a pike at the bottom of a winter pond. The world had shrunk to a cold ball of light, and the only thing to do was wait.

The matter-reducer was two huge rings above a lake of mercury. The rings were electric coils which somehow tricked the body as it lay on the mercury into a mass of greyish, doughy syrup looking like molten sodium. There was no more than half a litre of this, and it was quickly spooned off the mercury to avoid freezing it, and then containerised and sealed in something which looked suspiciously like a milk-bottling plant. The reduced matter still had to be kept chilled, otherwise it would heat up and reconvert. If this happened too quickly, then people would come back inside out. Nobody knew where the extra mass went or why the big rings could pry matter so neatly away from this dimension, but it meant that any number of Proles could be shipped cheaply into space. Some of them would come back left-handed, or with the distinct impression of having already lived their earthly lives. But these were all small prices to pay for the certainty of progress.

As Chrissie went into matter-reduction she felt a slight tickle, and her mood became less bleak. She enjoyed being poured into the stainless steel bottle. It felt safe in there. The only thing that could get her out of there would be *heat*. The automatic loaders took the racks of containers to the rockets which sat on the oily concrete deep underground. The launcher was a huge ramp pointed east, so the rockets could achieve escape velocity faster.

They had fat stubby wings so that they could glide down to earth again afterwards. The dirty, oil-streaked rockets were a shock to people who only saw torchings, which were done by a special, or the soap opera 'Safe Among The Stars', which was all done in the studio. The rockets had doors like bomb bays underneath for parking the Cryos in orbit. Some of them were older than Chrissie, and still used the old-fashioned methane boosters which had been brought in when oil ran out. The smell created by some of the older rockets was the only thing that had allowed the container stacking and loading to be done automatically, in these job-hungry times.

The freighter which was to carry Chrissie up to orbit was a particularly old rocket. Originally it had belonged to Mudroche, the Feely empire king, and had been used for freighting Feelies all over the world. Then Mudroche had sold it to the government and it had become the ZV-3. Before that, it had been *The Fair Viol*.

ZV-3 had a crew of five and was haunted by the smell of drains. There were two pilots, one of whom was the Captain, a gunner, a navigator, and a flight engineer. The whole business could have been performed unmanned, but the crews were kept on like the doctors, to provide a Caring Environment for Cryos. The state would have not been imaginative enough to take this step, but the cryogenic concept had been designed from scratch by a body of enormously influential men. Absolutely unknown to the general public, they were a far-sighted consortium of all the tv networks who had put up half the money for the Gatwick freezer plant, provided the government then used the old-fashioned freighters. The government agreed, old-fashioned freighters were built, and the consortium launched in parallel to the Cryo Programme the long-running hit serial of cryogenesis and the crews who ran the freighters, called 'Safe Among The Stars'. Fully 98.6 per cent of the nation watched it. Whenever one of the tv actors became ill, the 'secret' launchpad at Gatwick became surrounded by weeping women carrying comfits, books, home-made cake and flowers. Cryo boomed.

And the crews who worked the freighters had grown up with the series. By the time Chrissie had grown up and shot into orbit, the government could not have abandoned cryo without provoking a popular outcry.

On the day that *The Fair Viol* took off, there had been an episode on the tv where the cryo freighters had engaged with Russian fighters. The result was that the gunner, Pagey, was suddenly issued with a thousand rounds of live ammunition, which he had to carry and store in the gun turret. The ammo was brand new, gleaming, and extremely heavy. Pagey was paranoid and believed that the script had been deliberately written to start World War Three.

'This is just the beginning. You watch, they'll really be pushing the boat out soon. All started by some cunt sending round memos, trying to get themselves promotion, inside tv, asking for more *relevance*.'

Pagey was tall and gaunt with big bags under his eyes. He'd been on speed for years. He'd been engaged to Betty, the strangely placid radio operator. Betty hadn't said a thing when he called it off as suddenly as it had been on.

The inside of the ship was filthy. The pilot's seats were foam rubber bulging through plastic. The steering wheels were cracked plastic bound together with tape and string. In addition to the residual smell of methane fuel, the toilet had not been repaired for two flights. The Astroplex in the nose cone was cracked. It wasn't much like the tv series at all.

Pagey watched Betty clearing up. Pagey didn't help because none of the men did the clearing up on 'Safe Among The Stars'.

Betty was tall and slender and had big eyes. She was thirty-eight and a bachelor girl. She had an unhappy knack of falling for heavily married men then going off the idea of a relationship as soon as they were free of their other entanglements. But beyond this, and with her friends, she was discreet and loyal, wise and brave. She hadn't been overimpressed with her enormous good fortune when she landed the job of radio operator, so people said as they always had about Betty that she went through life in a dream. Betty had looked like a pinup girl for a long time but now, as cryo culled more and more volunteers in their forties, she was considered over the hill, far too old for more than a quick fling. When young flesh like Chrissie's was hurling itself off the planet with such alacrity, it was difficult to see what Betty had going for her once Pagey had turned her down after going up the back passage with her a few times. Not that Betty put herself about, either, or made any attempt to resnare the pill-fiend Pagey. Betty, extraordinarily, had some kind of Inner Calm, although she hadn't gone to any evening classes to centre on her Being. She wielded the vacuum-cleaner with its frayed lead without complaint.

Pagey turned and looked out of his gun-turret. A short stumpy figure was being pursued across the oily sodium-lit concrete apron by at least fifty photographers, towards the hull of ZV-3. It was Captain Punting, coming aboard after shore leave. His illegal metal-toed shoes clanged on the aluminium ladder and the noise echoed up and down the ship. Chrissie, a few degrees above absolute zero, felt it as a series of blissfully warming rippling vibrations which rocked her fluid, which went on for ever, like an Indian summer, kissing her awake again and again. Then the freezer in her stack came on again and she was borne away from the danger zone of consciousness, off her bed of lilies down to two hundred and fifty degrees below.

Captain Punting entered. A bloke had told him that there were still pubs on the London to Birmingham canal where you could get waterborne Guinness. Punting had arrived at the pubs two hundred years after they had stopped serving this particular delicacy with its unmatched head and fragrance, and had drunk a number of other beverages instead. Punting had a Drink Problem and had broken the ship's toilet. The drink made him untrustworthy, for having used it in such large quantities as a mantle against boredom and shyness for so many years, he was starting to suffer blackouts, and had forgotten what he was meant to have done that was so bad.

Punting's handlebar moustache was much sought after by photographers on that day, because it made him look like a *real* pilot, like one of the 'Safe Among The Stars' actors. In fact Punting usually allowed his number two to fly. He was involved with a religious crisis which had culminated in hallucinations in the toilet followed by a fierce, inconclusive battle with his own excrement. Coming aboard this time he had a large plastic cross round his neck and, more mysteriously, a 'lucky' fish which someone had given him in a pub.

Punting's coat had sleeves of encrusted braid which came down over his hands, issued in the same haste as Pagey's ammunition. It was in fact a captain's coat, but apart from Betty, who always wore the regulation hat, knee-length grey skirt and seamed black stockings, all the crew had grimy overalls with countless zips all over them. Punting generally topped his uniform off with a civilian touch such as brogues or an umbrella and bowler hat. This time however he had apparently been got at by some theatrical costumier. Not since opera designers ran up the styles for the Third Rcich had a cap had such a rake to the peak, hung about with sta-brite gold braid. Punting had a red round face, with a snub nose, short dark hair and baffled brown eyes. The *paparazzi* kept on flashing outside. They had found the ship's original name under a layer of paint. Mudroche would love to have his name linked to the protectors of Albion against the Russian scare, particularly as the latest Russian scare was his idea in the first place. The best picture of *The Fair Viol* would be printed big.

'Oh sir, you look a smasher in that coat. Go and show yourself.'

'Makes me look like a bloody commissionaire. I don't know why you have to dress up as a doorman in order to be killed. Anyway,' Punting added, 'I'm damned if I'm going to be killed. I've been through a few Russian scares in my time.'

The fan in Chrissie's stack went off again and the temperature began to climb dangerously. Chrissie experienced another awakening over aeons as the aluminium steps clanged again. This time Chrissie wasn't so pleased. She'd been sitting in her anger and the noise of the steps woke her understanding of the outside world and told her too much about it. Like a reluctant medium she vibrated to the second pilot, who was climbing the steps.

His name was Shorter and he was forty-five, and his vibrations announced that he was the very essence of suburban man, diligent, emotionally repressed, the father of grown-up children, who liked *pottering* in his greenhouse. Chrissie absorbed his receding hair, his punctuality, his small-mindedness which carried within it the core of self-righteous malice. Shorter weekly carried thousands of souls to perdition but didn't like sex or violence on tv. He was one of a small group of people who stood up against the Maltese when they opened a Videobuggery in Surbiton. Videobuggery was technically illegal, like cock-fighting, but the Enforcement had been cut in on the deal and no-one could stop it. Shorter thought of throwing a bomb in there but he disliked corpses, having found his mother dead when he was a child.

The fan stayed off. There was something wrong with the thermostat. Chrissie knew as much about the crew so far as they did about themselves and this was not comfortable knowledge. It was as if they were walking round her head trailing pictorial biographies. She felt Punting's bewilderment with the wretchedly full Portosan in both hands, afraid to go outside with it to confront photographers with an opportunity for humorous contrast to the grim fiction of *The Fair Viol* and her place in the front line against the Russian Scare. She felt Betty's irritation at her broken nail. All the feelings that were not actually part of their conscious thought-processes Chrissie had no choice but to experience. Their histories stretched behind them, into the dark of unconsciousness. There was Shorter as a small boy making a model of a space ship. And there two strands wove together for a moment as Betty and Pagey made love with all their clothes on, drifting over the heads of the other sleeping crew members, weightless in the dim blue light that crept through the plastic blinds shielding them from the everlasting day of solar orbit in space.

Then the ladder clanged again. This one was harder to read. There didn't seem to be any past to this one's character, and there wasn't a lot of future either. His name was Easey, and he was the new flight engineer.

In the cramped corridor above the hold, Easey met Punting with his load. Easey reacted to Punting's braid, and his big black face, frowning with eagerness to serve, banged on the roof as he tried to stand up and salute. Punting could just make out the whites of his eyes in the dark. Easey was extremely black. Punting had forgotten that they were getting a new engineer, but told him to go right in to the cabin and not be afraid. The coloured races always responded well to firm but kind handling. As Easey squeezed past him, Punting laid an affectionate hand on his shoulder and the cross tangled with Easey's spanking new repair box with his name on the top: JOHN BRINKLEY EASEY.

'Don't be afraid, Easey. Remember Christ has serviced your debts.' Easey was an amnesiac, and all of the past except for the last two years at engineering school was a complete blank to him. Easey would have happily embraced the doctrine of Original Sin and Christ's redemptive powers, but he had no notion of having come originally from anywhere. Easey's life had started when he had been washed ashore at Dunwich, in East Anglia. He had no clothes or memory or anything to trace him by. He had taken his name from the last relic on land of the drowned village of Dunwich, a single tombstone which stood on top of a crumbling cliff. Easey was gauche, for his social training only went back two years.

He went past Punting and entered the main cabin, to find himself in the middle of a discussion on free will. It had started when Betty had emptied the vacuum-cleaner into the Portosan and Punting had objected. Easey loved discussions. He especially liked to hear intelligent people talk. If he understood it correctly, the man with the flashing eyes and PAGE, ENGNNR. on his suit was saying that the bulk of any vacuuming of a confined space such as a cabin would be discarded skin cells from all personnel therein, and so it followed that even the distinguished Captain would have made a contribution to household dust and should do his share of the removal of the same. Then the woman went back to cleaning and the man with the flashing eyes included him in the discussion without introducing himself or asking Easey's name. Easey was flattered and gave Pagey's argument, which was for biological determinism, a sympathetic hearing.

'We're like skin cells,' Pagey was saying. 'We're unimportant to the main thrust of events in the universe. We're endlessly discarded. Nobody knows when they're going to die an' skin cells don't know when they're going to die, and it's a good job skin cells don't have free will or else they'd never die and you'd end up like a bleeding tortoise or armadillo with a shell half a mile thick. And do you know why we don't know when we're going to die?'

Easey hadn't yet worked out how he was born so he let Pagey carry on with his fascinating speculation. What an original mind he had! What fine calf muscles the young woman had! He was surprised that she did not pay as much attention to the man as his conversation suggested he deserved. And here he came again.

'All forms of life are simply vehicles for the survival of DNA. That's all we are. Milkfloats for a fucking genetic archetype. It's *pathetic*. DNA doesn't care if there's a war. DNA doesn't care if we fuck up the whole planet, because in a couple of million years the radiation level will drop and DNA will seed the planet again from all those meteorites which are chockful of fucking organic compounds floating in space. And another thing,' said Pagey.

'The whole Cryogenetics Programme isn't a human idea at all. It's another wheeze from up the sleeve of DNA. Even if cryo was run properly, an' everybody knows we're really just flushing them down the khazi, even if they come back, there's still going to be the same problem. The problem bugging everybody is, how do you survive under the slavedriving of DNA?'

Then the quiet man with the pipe in the corner spoke up without turning round from watering his geraniums. He said something quite crushing to Pagey which Easey thought would have clinched it. He said that Pagey's arguments were so old that he'd forgotten the answers to them. This was exactly the kind of stimulating talk that Easey needed to catch up on his missing years. He made some mental notes. 'Deeyennay' was obviously new slang for God. 'Fucking' he knew meant extremely, 'fuck' meant mess. Easey did not know any other meanings for the word.

He had studied engineering and nothing else and so all pro-creation was a closed book to him.

Chrissie was drifting off again when Punting decided to solve the problem of the photographers and the soil bucket by simply pouring the waste matter into the hold amongst the cryos. He broke the lead seal with his penknife and opened the hatch. There was plenty of space between the bottles and crates. The nitrogen swirled around the stacks, making it look like a tiny foggy library viewed from above. It was illegal to break the seal and in response to the warmer air all the cooling fans burst into life. Punting had begun to pour the container when the wet rim touched the top of a crate and froze, bonding it instantly. Punting wrenched it off, then as in a nightmare realised that he had lost his balance and was going to fall into the hold. He left one shoe behind and toppled into the gap between the stacks after the Portosan, which the crew had purchased with a whip-round after his little accident. Relaxed by the Gordon's, and buffered by his oversize coat, Punting came to rest upside down, and knew he had to act fast if he was to live. He turned round and wriggled his way up the stacks till he got to the top, out of breath. The hatch was only a couple of feet away. He grabbed at a crate to pull himself out and his hand stuck round a container. He yanked the bottle out of its crate and rolled sideways out of the hold, and shut the hatch.

He was alive, but he appeared to be married to a matter-reduction bottle which wouldn't come off his hand. In the bottle was Chrissie.

While Chrissie was cool, she was happy. But Punting's hand was living, warm, wrapping her round with rough, searing fire, jerking the temperature of the thin-walled flask up by leaps and bounds. Punting, however, just felt his hand freezing.

In the cabin they had heard the noise as Punting fell in and clambered out again. 'Fuck! Fuck!' he had shouted, to Easey's approval. Everyone seemed pleased that he had fallen in the hold and Easey smiled too. Nobody made any move to help him. Shorter simply said that he should sober up at minus two fifty, and Pagey had said it was the finger of Deeyennay beckoning Punting

49

into the indefinite future. There would come a time, Pagey prophesied, when Punting's delirium tremens and personality disintegration would be exactly what life in the universe would need to get launched in a new direction, and certainly Deeyennay would then see to it that Punting would unfreeze.

Punting came back in with a light dusting of frost, and his hand deep in his coat pocket, hiding a grimace of pain behind his moustache. As soon as he sat down in the pilot's seat the pain forced him to cry out and he pulled his hand out of his pocket, still nursing the bottle.

Inside the bottle Chrissie understood what was happening from the reactions in present time of the crew. Betty was radioing ground control trying to get them to cancel the launch, but they were on work to rule.

'Afraid I had a slight prang. Nearly got trapped by the shit freezing me to the wall. Hope I don't lose my hand.'

Chrissie would happily have bitten his hand off at the wrist if she could in order to get back in the stack. She felt the heat and the anger rising together. She felt she was going to explode. She didn't want to explode.

Betty called and called but to no avail. Everyone was getting nervous by now. There was always a risk to anyone in the vicinity if a canister exploded.

'Hello Gatwick this is ZV-3. Priority call, request permission to cancel launch.' But the answering airwaves were empty. Everyone looked at Punting. Punting felt the weight of their collective hostility, and began to drift bravely towards the door to the hold, as if he'd thought of it first as the gentlemanly thing to do. But he didn't go out. He held his arm round the door and pressed himself up against the inside. The next few minutes were going to be a mite tense. It was rotten bad luck he'd had that prang.

Sir, she is a fair viol, and your sense the strings,
Who fingered to make man his lawful music,
Would draw heaven down and all the gods to hearken.
                                    –From *Pericles, Prince of Tyre*, attributed
                                                to William Shakespeare

Punting's soused blood kept trying to get through the capillaries to his hand, but his heart wasn't up to it yet. However in the end the alcohol won, the capillaries reopened and the blood started to creep in and around the capsule to carry the cold away.

In the spring, the old stories go, the young spring sun, the fiery hero, melts the snow princess out of her prison of ice, where she has been awaiting her deliverer. Chrissie's prison allowed her to be privy to the situation of her rescue and she became determined on one thing. She was going to stay in her dream and never be rescued.

The bottle got warmer and warmer, and Chrissie got more and more determined that she was never going to go back into *that* world. Easey asked Pagey what was going to happen, in a whisper.

'There's going to be this fleshy explosion. All the windows will blow out, and Puntin' will be left with the raw stump of his arm up some fifteen-stone psychopath's arse. The rest of us, all dead, from Eternity Shock.'

Betty was still trying to get through to ground control five minutes later when Punting slowly lowered his arm and walked back to the pilot's seat. Shorter moved away discreetly.

'I am not . . . going to apologise for this capsule. It is perfectly safe, even at room temperature.' Punting liturgically repeated the government's handouts on canisters, but nobody who didn't have to ever believed anything that came out of the Ministry of Space.

'Put it back in the hold, Punting,' Pagey said firmly.

'I have no intention of being eternally frozen to please you lot. This capsule is quite safe and I am quite prepared to fly the ship holding it.' They had a double green to join the queue at the bottom of the ramp and Shorter had seen them taking the chocks away. How anyone could fly with a frosting cocktail shaker in one hand that might at any moment explode with a roar of blood and guts was difficult for Easey to understand, but the launching was all done automatically, like all the difficult bits.

There was a rumour that the physical events of reconversion were affected by the phases of the moon. And yet Bunce, who had been torched on the full moon for maximum impact, had made hardly a splash. The Burning Judge had been puzzled by this until he had made some astrological computations, and worked out that it was when the moon was dark that the torchings had flared in technicolour in the corona of the sun. This explanation had satisfied him and he had resolved to pay more attention to detail on torchings. (Not that the law waited: young Carwash had been caught red-handed in a cryo plant and there was no question but that he'd be torched on peak viewing, whatever other factors there were, just as soon as the trusties could pry him off the floor they'd quick-frozen him to. He would be a visual flop, too.)

Shorter had seen a multiple conversion once. The incident had been unreported, but a freezer motor had failed on a cryo freighter before launching, the next ship in line for takeoff up the ramp. There was a distant, irregular popping, like aerosol cans exploding in a fire, and then the emergency access door at the base of the hold sprang off as smartly as if it had been opened by explosive bolts and, in a nightmare vision horrible to relate, a pinkish gooey mass began to nudge its way on to the apron, looking rather like sausagemeat. The ship had been towed out of the queue, and men in gumboots had hosed down the apron with detergent.

It had been a full moon then too.

Shorter didn't want to take any chances, and so he drew the sturdy vinyl screen across that separated the pilots from the rest of the crew, and went to join Betty and Pagey, as far away from Punting as was possible in the cramped cabin. He didn't want to frighten them.

'It's all right. I've seen reconversion, dozens at a time.' Pagey asked what it was like. Shorter looked him in the eye. 'Popcorn.'

Behind the plastic screen with its cheerful plastic ducks glued on by Betty, Punting was filled with the reckless courage that

53

convinces the entirely drunk that they are fit to drive. The capsule had concentrated his mind wonderfully, acting as a frosty tonic. As the launching was mostly automatic the only danger came if the capsule broke the pilots' window, which was already cracked. But Punting was happily prepared to risk his life and everybody else's as he watched the automatic countdown, wiggling the flaps and the ailerons manually and redundantly, just like the old days. If the big window in front of him went, well then, as the Scots used to say, it was goodnight Vienna, and you wouldn't have more than fifteen seconds to curse your luck in space, before signing off for good. Still it was a very large window, a round one, and the crack was rather large. Punting began to wish he'd paid more attention to it when they'd had a proper flight engineer, and had had him log it in for a replacement. But there was no point in worrying about it now.

'Crew to positions.' The G-forces up the ramp and through the huge hoops were massive but brief. The crew decided to stay lying on the padded rear bulkhead. Shorter found himself standing by Easey, who was slowly moving his huge protuberant eyes like a sleepy frog. Pagey mimed shooting himself in the head. Suddenly the lights went out. Punting spoke again.

'When I turn the lights on again I want to see you all sitting in your seats. There'll be no recriminations if you act now, understand? The countdown is rolling now.'

There was a pause. Betty buckled herself into her chair hurriedly. There was no room on the bulkhead for her.

'I take it you're all in your seats. Good. Six, five four three.' There was a thump as the brake pads came off and the ship began to inch forward. The methane rockets came on stream with a distant grinding shriek, underneath the noise of a thousand kettles boiling. 'Two, one, rolling zero countdown, all systems A-OK –' Punting may have said something else but the noise level went up as all three methane boosters went on stream, to the familiar miaowing bellow, and the nose went up, the duck-covered curtain flew open to show light at the end of the ramp, a tiny circle which grew and grew while the numerous small objects which had not

54

been secured rained painfully on the crew on the bulkhead. Then suddenly they were in daylight, climbing under the rocket's own power, with the outside air temperature already fifty degrees below zero, and the sky a richer darker blue than you could see anywhere on earth. The duck curtain gradually settled again to the ship's own gravity system, as the acceleration lessened, and the hunched figure of Punting in front of the big window with all the dawning stars was hidden again.

Easey closed his eyes and thanked Deeyennay for a safe takeoff. Chrissie in her capsule was not aware that they had taken off, for the world already seemed like a small ball of daylight, and in space it wasn't much different. She concentrated on resisting the heat of Punting's hand, but the battle was being slowly lost. A series of audible clicks, like an icecube in warm water, started coming from the canister. The ship climbed out past the moon, the great governess of fertility. The moon was already on the wane. The ship passed her great bright face and, using the gravitational field as a child might swing round a lamp-post and go off in a different direction, *The Fair Viol* heave-ho'ed round the dark side. Pagey watched Earthset from the gunner's window.

They were meant to store the canisters in a parking orbit round the earth and here Punting had taken them round the dark side of the moon already. And suddenly Punting had left the controls as they climbed away from the moon's gravity in a different direction, and was amongst them, with the canister in his hand. Chrissie's disembodied awareness reached out desperately in the surrounding space for a lever to help her stay in cryo. Shorter meanwhile had sneaked a look at the fuel gauges. Punting had pushed them up to fully a quarter of the speed of light, and they were almost empty. The ship had apparently been pointed back along the solar system's track in space.

'It's perfectly all right,' Punting said. 'It's so that nothing would happen to my hand. You see, if we keep on this course, all the astrological influences will be arrested and so nothing untoward can happen.' The fuel gauges were showing empty. Their speed was beyond rescue. The canister clicked.

Chrissie felt the moon shrinking away, and the spaceship moving away from the other planets, the friends of the earth, in their courtly dance round the sun, and she became aware that they were leaving the solar system. Cryo no longer felt so comfy. And now suddenly in matter-reduction she became aware of the planets talking, in strange singsong voices as if they had just breathed helium. They were talking to her:

Oh oh oh oh
Space Queen

What, me? Chrissie replied

Oh oh oh oh
Space Queen

There seemed to be a lot of planets trying to talk to her. They called her all sorts of nice names, and Chrissie thought she would tell them her problem, which was that she wanted to stay in cryo.

No way, sister! Any moment now and you're going to pop back out.

The inner planets seemed to be in a bunch, giggling like children, while Saturn, with the rings, and three others she didn't recognise stayed aloof. Although she was careering away from the solar system, the planets seemed to be getting closer and closer to her. Chrissie had not taken any interest in the solar system except as a repository for herself until *The Future*! arrived, and was irritated at the planets' cheerfulness and animation. There was a tune going too. Chrissie, who had loved to dance once, got angry.

If you get angry you will blow, said one of the outer planets. It was Uranus. Neptune kept playing the music.

No way, No way, No way

Chrissie felt the pain of frustration and anger goading her like red hot needles. Even in cryo, it seemed, you could break down and weep. Then, through her tears, she saw the planets do a strange thing. All at once, to the music of Neptune, they made a line abreast around the sun, pointing straight at Aries.

Shorter was too careful to hurry about leading a revolt but he said, shaking his head, that if they all got back alive, there was *no way* Punting could keep his licence. Punting, back behind the flying duck screen by popular request, was working out with his left hand, since his right was full of canister, that they had *easily* enough fuel left to return, when the canister detached itself from his hand and fell on the floor. He sprang out, first to tell the good news to the crew, and next to relieve himself into the hold and rescue his shoe, leaving the canister in the co-pilot's seat. Pagey yelled at him to come and get it and put it back or they'd turn the gravity off, but everyone knew that the gravity was automatic and Punting took his time, enjoying the gradual ebbing of pain from his bladder after all the excitement, and taking care, in a fair-minded way, to spread it about a bit in the hold. He didn't want to heat up a capsule, just in case there had been a ghastly mistake and some of them weren't safe at room temperature. Feeling for his shoe, Punting missed his footing and fell upside down into the hold again. Suddenly there was a noise like a tumble drier starting up, and even less explicably, a zig-zag zebra of light floated round the narrow passage and vibrated to the noise. *This is it*, thought Punting. *This is the fatal heart attack*, and he hurriedly buttoned his flies. There were some things that a chap didn't like to leave undone.

In the cabin, Easey had been trying to rescue the container with a piece of coat-hanger wire when the noise and the zebra lights happened. He continued to fish for the canister until he got a violent electric shock from it up the coat-hanger wire which made him cry out. The light pattern was all about the cabin, and the crew were disorientated and dizzy as if they'd stood up suddenly, having sat down too long. From the hold came a distant thump, as the dizziness overtook Punting and he fell down among the stacks. Then there was a kind of squeaky pop, and the zebra lines broke down into an infinitely fine texture then disappeared. For a moment it looked as if everything was not substantial but simply had the picture of matter drawn on it and cleverly coloured in.

Then it slowly cleared, and everything went back to normal. Only, Betty felt that it was *more* normal than usual if anything. There didn't seem much to worry about beyond her broken nail. So none of them was in the least upset except Pagey, who had had some bad experiences with acid, when the whole of the fabric of the visible world started to be drawn in towards Chrissie's capsule.

There are sheets in rich men's houses, it is said, fine enough to be drawn through a wedding ring. And it was in this manner that *The Fair Viol* went through the portal of Chrissie's capsule, and out the other side, where instead of fleeing the solar system they were approaching it at the same speed as they had left it. And there was another major difference, which was that all the planets were politely lined up between the constellation of Aries and the sun. Only the earth's moon was poking its head out of the line, like a dog sticking its head out between soldiers' legs at a parade. Chrissie, in the strength of her desire not to reconvert, had pulled herself and her surroundings into a parallel universe, similar enough to escape detection at first, with the exception of the deployment of the planets.

Chrissie noticed that her mermaid tights which she'd brought bundled up for good luck had turned into a cornucopia of fishy things. Behind the screen, still with the flying ducks on it, Chrissie lay dressed in the full tv Xmas spectacular mermaid costume which she'd coveted, and arranged round her on ledges were plastic prawns, lobsters and carp, and even a John Dory with its hideous gaping head. She was alive and well and looking like a fishmonger's dream. But she was in a very black mood. She hadn't wanted to come back *anywhere*, even dressed as a tv star.

It was Pagey who drew the curtain to find out where this trip was going. There'd been a reconversion but the main window had survived. He had to stifle a laugh when he saw what had come back though. He bowed ceremoniously and indicated her to the rest of the crew, like a waiter asking them to be seated.

'Popcorn, anyone?' he asked. Betty glanced at him and turned back to try and raise Gatwick, without success. Shorter slipped into Punting's seat, since his own was full, and gazed out along the line of planets. The fuel gauges still read empty even after he tapped them and the ship was still gaining speed even with its engines turned off. There was no denying this was a puzzle which he'd have to solve on his own in the absence of Punting. Shorter reached across Chrissie for his matches and struck a Vesta on an abalone shell which seemed to have appeared on the console. He quickly crumbled some Three Nuns into his pipe and lit it in order to study the problem better. There was no doubt that it was a rum one.

The universe into which *The Fair Viol* had been accidentally drawn by Chrissie's desires had not answered her own wishes to be kept *en bouteille*, and it was not the paradise of eternal gratification which Chrissie imagined was in store for her in the distant future. Earth was more or less similar to the Earth which the space crew had just left. The Burning Judge still presided over solar immolations. Cryogenics was used by the state to cure its problems. And Carwash was going to die that afternoon, for attacking a cryo plant. The judge would have no difficulty in deciding sentence.

You, Carwash, are a bitter lesson to the state. You were placed in a position of trust and responsibility and used it deliberately to plan a series of assaults on life and property which had they been entirely successful would have led to the complete collapse of the state as we know it. You have betrayed your friends and your country. I can think of only one punishment which would adequately express the public repugnance which all classes of society have expressed, and I shall overrule counsel's plea for insanity. The act was cruelly calculated. The man must answer for it. I sentence you to be taken from here and cryogenically frozen while still living. You will then be matter-reduced, and placed in one of Her Majesty's Freighters . . .

In both universes, the sales of Sleepiwake soared.

The Burning Judge turned off the lights in the studio in both universes after having sent old Carshaw's son down. It hurt him to do it but he couldn't go soft on anarchy now. He thought how fine it would be to retire from the world here, away from that malevolent will o' the wisp, the law, away from a sick state, from doctors who were not doctors, and Enforcement huggermugger with the worst kinds of drug rings and violent criminals, and the spavined unions, who every day saw more of their members betrayed. But he never regretted his decision to be a judge, although his contribution had been made in difficult days. He hung up his robes and wig in the cupboard where the sherry was, and took the bottle upstairs. It was time to tup the stusher.

Upstairs the stusher stared at him strangely, without undressing. She had taken an overdose of sleeping pills. The judge shook his head.

'I don't understand this at all. You had a perfectly good job.'

He hated her when she looked at him like that, a dowdy, dumpy little secretary who had got too close. 'Tell me if you're in trouble, but there are some cries for help I'd rather not hear.' And then the tears had started on down her cheeks. The judge called the butler to fetch the stomach pump, right away. The judge kept one against poisoning.

In ZV-3, Punting was still upside down in the hold, and Betty was having no luck putting out the call sign. Shorter reached over Chrissie again to feel the soil in his geranium which he kept above his seat. Easey was trying to hold the worn floor covering down with a pop riveter. He had his head right next to the ground and his huge bottom was getting in everybody's way. Pagey toed it to one side to get to his guns. However when Easey finally looked up he didn't say a word about that, he just said he wasn't happy at all with the state of the pilot's *video unit*. Pagey couldn't believe his ears at the language of this black boy and stared at him openmouthed till Easey dropped his torque wrench.

Pagey asked him if he knew that engineers, even *coon* engineers, weren't supposed to get in the way of the lovely Betty when she was doing her important job.

'What is a coon?' Easey asked interestedly. People had shouted the word at him in the street, as if they were trying to tell him something. Pagey said he didn't know what a coon was either, they'd always been a bit of a mystery to him as well, but he was pretty sure Easey was a coon.

'For a start, Easey, you're black. An' that gives you a head start on being initiated into the mysteries of being a coon.' Easey thanked him and repeated his remark about the video unit. 'It's been like that for two flights. Did they teach you to call it that at engineering school?' Easey's engineering school had been both mother and father to him and he nodded.

'It's funny how they keep changing the names of things. Did they tell you at engineering school that you were going to end up shovelling shit? Because that's the major problem, Easey. The khazi's bust. That never happens on "Safe Among The Stars", does it? That section of your job is not in the public interest. The last engineer got a transfer to avoid doing anything about it. But I'm afraid it's your province.'

Betty kept calling Gatwick without success. Shorter studied a star map for a while before realising that he was holding it upside down. He felt strangely warm and sleepy. They had made a jump somehow in space and they weren't at all where they were supposed to be. Still, as long as Betty followed the Instructions Procedure, no one could blame them. He turned the star map the right way up, and tried to think what had happened to Punting. Punting had gone out to relieve himself. Punting was always going off for nips and naps anyhow, so it was hard to get worried.

Chrissie hated these people with a passion born of pure dread. It was like waking to find yourself still in a cruel dream in the real world. The curious thing about the crew though was that none of them was noticing her, and she thought if she kept very still that the dream might fade. And so she sat hardly daring to blink, praying that Punting would not come back.

Betty gave up calling Gatwick and tried to make Easey feel a bit more at home, asking him where he came from.

'I'm amnesiac, I can't remember anything before engineering school. I tried to find out, but there are so many people missing on the cryo programme.'

'Poor bastard. As if being born black wasn't enough, he has to be born an amnesiac prole,' Pagey said.

'I don't think you're right. I think I might find out one day that I was the son of a judge, or the Minister for Space.'

This boy really does have a thick skin, thought Pagey. He actually said he wanted to be one of *them*.

'At least I'm not out of work.' Easey looked straight past Chrissie at Shorter, there being nothing in flight regulations for engineers about mermaids.

'Could I get at the video unit please? I should have checked it already.' Easey tried to squeeze himself between Chrissie and Shorter. Chrissie tensed. Shorter held up an arm. The poor lad was so green, he couldn't even tell when he wasn't wanted. Shorter almost felt sorry for him, except it was his sort that had brought the country to its knees in his opinion.

'Could you just hold off for a bit, Sunny Jim, till I've found out where we are?' Engineers always thought they owned the place. But the Z series were so simple to operate that the job was a piece of window dressing, even more so than the gunner. Though to tell the truth, Shorter wasn't upset to be flying with a gunner during the most recent Russian scare. The Russians thought that the West was storing cryogenic armies in space, and whenever there was a flap, cryo freighters got buzzed. Shorter wondered how long it would take to teach Sunny Jim his place. From the way he was reacting to Pagey's broad hints, it'd be some time.

Shorter looked out on the line of planets with his binoculars. He could make out the nearer ones up to Saturn easily, with the naked eye, but then there were the darker spheres of Uranus, Neptune and Pluto, where the sunlight was decidedly thin. He had seen the planets moving erratically to their present positions as they entered the second universe, the great globes pulsing like fireflies through the striations in the cracked glass of the nose. He beckoned to Pagey, who stood looking through the binoculars, next to Chrissie. Chrissie could smell Pagey quite clearly. Pagey was a man who liked to keep his black sweatshirts on for some time.

I'm dreaming I'm smelling someone, thought Chrissie. Pagey obligingly moved away. *I am controlling this dream*, thought Chrissie. But she could still smell him and Pagey wasn't about to move away any farther. He was looking out of the window.

'Bloody hell. You're right. All the planets, lined up like a trick billiard shot.' Pagey handed the binoculars back. 'When did that last happen?'

'Never. And it shouldn't be happening now.' Pagey's interest in the mystery died quickly and he was about to ask Shorter whether he was aware that there was a young mermaid in the other seat, prior to engaging the returnee from matter-reduction in some light banter, when Betty got a reply from Gatwick.

'ZV-3, this is Gatwick. We can't fix your position. We're barely reading you. Can you give us a coordinate?' Then, because they were on work to rule, they switched over to broadcasting a Wurlitzer instrumental version of 'Strangers in the Night'. Shorter said it would be a fair bit yet before he had worked out the coordinates, but he'd be happy if Betty left the music on. Betty started doing her nails again. Pagey drifted back to the gun emplacement and started re-reading *Mad* magazines with a serious expression. Chrissie was relieved. She didn't want to be investigated, and she knew that she was something to do with the lineup of planets out there.

It had been a live recording from the Tower Ballroom, Blackpool, broadcast by the BBC, it turned out. Control must have been relaying it. It was generally hard to get the BBC in space. Next, there was a surprise. 'Memory Motorway', a radio programme which opened up brief and exciting vistas of the past with reminiscences from oldsters, had as its guest speaker a long-serving freighter pilot with the Cryogenic Programme, a rogue and alcoholic backslider, secret twirler of his moustache ends with his own earwax, Captain Punting himself.

'I thought we were having a sort of rest from Punting,' said Pagey. Betty left the radio and Chrissie started to panic. She was trying by sheer willpower to keep Punting out so that the dream would fade without her having to move out of her seat, and here he was trying to come back in via the radio. She had hated that man who had held her in his hand. She wanted him to die, in the stacks.

'I was flying fish when I left the RAF. Some chap had cornered the market and we were carrying a load of matter-reduced mackerel. We

were carrying it in one of the old "Y" freighters which as you probably recall had rear opening cargo doors. And the matter-reduced mackerel were in this box with a big freezer unit on it, lashed on to the rollers. It had about a thousand cubic yards of fish inside I'd say. So we were going to Australia, and over India this MIG 43 jumped me out of the sun. I couldn't outmanoeuvre him because I was so overweight. And he sat there, right on my tail. Most uncomfortable feeling, particularly as it was a tense time in the cold war and he had some very ugly looking rockets tied to the tummy of the MIG, he was really close. I could have almost reached out and cut him with my penknife, except we were a hundred and fifty miles up in the air.

So the next time he came up close to the cabin I stuck my tongue out at him. In those days it was the custom to have your country's flag tattooed on your tongue. He still stayed too close even after I had got out my wet Union Jack, so I decided to play a trick on him. I turned off the cooler motors on the fish, and opened the rear cargo doors.'

Punting's voice paused naturally in the middle of the story, which had been polished to perfection by years of recitation in pubs, cafés and aircrew transit buses, indeed anywhere which had a captive audience. But Punting knew how to hold his radio audience as well – it was like talking to chaps, but in the dark – and continued after the breathing space.

'Almost immediately, the fish started reconverting back out of reduced matter, boiling over the sides of the box, and pouring in a thick flood of hake and mackerel right in the MIG's trajectory. He went straight into this wall of fish and stopped dead in his tracks. I left him there and went suborbital over Borneo and about half the fish followed me out of orbit. But the other half stayed up with him and I could see the crew of the MIG out with repair suits, carrying buckets and filling them up with Dover Sole from their clogged air intakes.'

The interviewer asked Punting if he had ever read anything about rains of fishes but Punting would not be budged from telling the story as he always told it.

'They were you see collecting fish because they never had any fresh. Their base was in the Urals and they were thousands of miles from the sea. See?'

The reception went away and didn't come back. Betty yawned and stretched.

'I'm just going to *die* soon if I don't get a cigarette,' she said. Shorter took a plant sprayer and squirted his geranium carefully, and before putting the sprayer away again he absent-mindedly sprayed Chrissie. Suddenly he realised what he was doing and stopped. Pagey asked him what he thought he was doing. Shorter struggled to explain.

'Isn't she meant to be a mermaid?'

'It's a falsie,' Pagey replied contemptuously, pointing at the shimmering plastic scales and the elasticated waistband of her lower half.

'I didn't imagine it was *surgical*,' Shorter replied huffily. He surveyed the collection of plastic fish round her which had suddenly materialised in the jump from the one universe to the other, and shook his head. 'Poor little brat. Why d'you think she took this lot with her to face the next world?' The plastic fish and the parsley stuck on between them seemed the most wonderful thing to Easey suddenly, as did Chrissie's white vinyl handbag stuffed to overflowing with toy shrimps. Easey's confusion about procreation resolved itself when he decided that everybody, like him, had arrived and been born directly from the sea. Chrissie's sudden appearance ceased to be a surprise.

'She's *beautiful*,' he said admiringly. Pagey couldn't take the strain any more and popped a couple of pills, which seemed to have all their old buzz. He started speeding, crackling with ideas and paranoias, reckless and timid all at once.

'What do you think the chances are that she's your long-lost sister, Easey?' Pagey asked. But the sarcasm was lost on Easey, who stared at Chrissie spellbound. 'Don't let me stop you if you fancy having a quick wiggle. Except they've stopped one thing.

You can't turn the gravity off in these. Betty and I did it once like that. You should try it if you get the chance.'

Easey had fallen in love with Chrissie in the purest way possible. He was completely smitten, now he noticed her. It didn't seem to matter how she had come there. For him she had appeared as a responding cry to the agony of his heart. He had now found his beloved and felt a little more secure about talking about country matters. Couples he knew went together to places.

'Are you stepping out with Betty? I didn't realise you were engaged. Congratulations.' Pagey ignored this, but spoke to Easey in a loud, friendly way. It wouldn't do Betty any harm to get to hear the message again.

'No. My mum doesn't approve of career women, she says it would be much better for my career if I married a girl straight from school. I can see her point. With space girls you always end up washing your own socks.' Pagey's mum had been dead for years but Pagey still found her useful. 'You'd get along with my mum. She owns a three-bedroom semi in Hounslow.'

Easey was impressed. Plainly then Betty must be involved with someone else. Easey's mind was so full of his own love that he couldn't imagine anyone actually choosing to be out of love, once they got in it.

Shorter crossed over from the pilot's console and with his green fingers, succour to wilting plants, he started to work on Betty's shoulder and neck muscles. Betty hung her head back with a little moan of pleasure and Easey looked away hastily, as if he had been caught spying through a keyhole. So that was the couple, Shorter and Betty. But then Shorter stopped and walked away as if nothing had occurred between them and Betty put on a deep red lipstick before deciding against it and wiping it off with a lot of tissue. They had had a warning against massage parlours at the school. Easey wondered if what he'd just seen was *deep* massage, which was said to be more expensive than the other kind. But these people were so sophisticated they did it to each other in public without blinking, even though they were lost in space.

'Where *are* we going, Shorter?' Betty asked. She was rethreading her earrings through holes specially made in her ears. Chrissie had holes in her ears too, Easey saw, and it made him excited just to look and see things being pushed through.

Shorter sprawled in the captain's seat and tried casually to move the controls. You could move the joystick around a little but it always came back to the same place. Shorter shrugged.

'We popped up close to the sun, and we're on a track which takes us out parallel with the planets. We've passed Mercury, and now we're going past Venus. As to where we'll end up, I expect we'll know that when we get there.' He shook the joystick again. It was quite firm. Easey looked out of the window and looked again. Out there, keeping track with the ship, was something that looked like sunlight through rippling water on sand, or perhaps it was more like frilly green pillowcases swimming alongside of them. If you reported things like this at engineering school they sent you for an eye checkup, because it was important that everybody be taught to see the same things. If you saw anything else, it was deemed not to have happened, to be below the event threshold.

And then something else happened that shouldn't have happened. The radio came to life again and a trim, old-fashioned voice started to say, 'Germany calling. Germany calling.' It was the call sign used by German propaganda in the Second World War, before even Punting had been born. Pagey knew about Lord Haw-Haw, from the war comix. He'd been torched as a traitor to England, although he was in fact Irish. He'd either been trapped in a time warp or was being rebroadcast by the BBC. Easey asked Pagey whether the things he was seeing out of the window were real, or not. Pagey sat at his guns, hunting for phenomena.

'There's only one way to find out for sure whether things exist on this plane. Let's see if this bleeding ravioli's bulletproof.' Pagey fed a twenty-metre belt into the guns over the old condensed-milk tin he had taped to the side to stop the breech fouling during practice rounds. He fired it off and the smell of cordite arose and was swept away into the air cleaner. Easey reported that the green things had now gone. 'Now all we need to know is why we're getting *that* on the radio. It's probably a Kraut package tour to the asteroid belt, and they can't get their beer hall inflated.' Easey nodded, relieved. Pagey seemed to have an answer for everything.

Shorter felt the controls again. In spite of Pagey's machine-gunning the ship held rock steady on the same course. It wasn't normal, and he said so. Betty nodded encouragingly in agreement. *When I'm gone it'll be back to normal*, Chrissie thought. But this dream had been going on for too long.

Pagey had had one pill too many and screamed at Shorter and Betty and shouted that *he* was normal, and what's more he didn't have to prove he was normal. This took everyone by surprise. Pagey thought that the whole situation had been invented to get at him, and made a complete idiot of himself. He screamed that he was normal, it was just that he didn't want to get married. Shorter was normal. Shorter's geranium was normal. Betty was a normal stupid woman. Easey was an amnesiac normal. Pagey hit Easey on the shoulder in manic camaraderie of normality. Easey buckled, rather startled, but was pleased to be touted however loudly as normal. Pagey stuck his face in Betty's and asked her to define her version of normality, if she could. Betty said it was what was happening in the world they had just left, that was normal, and what was happening now wasn't normal. Betty was painting her nails now and pointed the brush at Chrissie. Chrissie was caught staring at her and quickly looked away but it gave Betty an opportunity.

'Is *she* normal?' Everyone stared at Chrissie. Pagey said, yes, to want to be a mermaid, and get away from this rotten stinking shitty world, yes, it's *normal*. As long as everybody realised that everything was normal, everyone would be all right. With that, Pagey sat down at his guns, grey in the face with fatigue after running an anger jag on top of everything else. He hadn't meant to say that at all. He knew it was Chrissie who was causing everything, but the rest were too stupid to see the danger. He'd have to bide his time and try and get her on his own.

It was Shorter who said that Betty looked as tired as he felt, and that maybe they'd all be better for a little sleep. He turned everything out except the blue combat light, and settled down to sleep. Easey, as if hypnotised, drooped over the toolbox and started to snore softly. Betty put a frown mask on to stop her wrinkles and clicked up all the old-fashioned brass toggles on the radio, to give the valves a chance to cool off. Chrissie herself began to drift towards the borders of sleep. *Oh good, this is the end of this horrid dream*, she thought.

The judge lay in his huge bed, with linen so fine you could thread the sheet through a wedding ring. The butler had pumped the stusher's stomach out and she was sleeping downstairs. At the hour of the wolf, the moon came out and shone on the floor beside the judge's bed. He was still furious with the stusher, and if the butler hadn't been there he would have had a good mind to teach her a lesson with his rhinoceros whip. He lay in bed, his mind a mathematical playground of sadism. He would cut her up and barrow the pieces over to the swine. No. Too much blood. He would drug her semi-conscious and put her on the lawn and watch as she was pursued and finally mangled by the robot grass cutter. Unlikely. She'd done it deliberately to annoy him. He toyed with the idea of burning the house down around her, or keeping her locked up in the old pantry like a wild animal. Then she might show a bit of gratitude.

The temperature of the room dropped a few degrees as the ghost of the house's builder drifted up the stairs and through the wall where the old door had been. It had been his children's nursery, and some undischarged anxiety would draw the phantom back again and again till demolition. He was familiar to the judge, who did not fear death, since he believed that judges went to a different place to the rest of humanity. But tonight he could not sleep, and he put up the electric blanket another point – how warmth flees from the old! – and set about wondering about the stusher again. At first he had wanted to fire her, at such an obvious attempt at blackmailing for sympathy: because she shared his bed for half an hour occasionally didn't mean he was going to make a good woman of her.

A white figure appeared at the door. The judge hadn't seen the ghost that close for a long time. But the illusion vanished when the white figure sat heavily on the bed. It was the stusher, coming to apologise. The judge pretended he was asleep. The stusher climbed into bed beside him and whispered she was sorry, she hadn't wanted to involve him in any way, but the fact was she was pregnant.

Overhead, in both universes, the stars continued in their courses.

Chrissie woke with a start from her sleep to find herself still in the same place, and Pagey standing over her, jerking at her mermaid skin as if they were in the back row of the Peckham Odeon, but although everybody else was asleep, it turned out he wasn't after *that*.

'All right, what's the game? Are you human, or some fucking alien?' Chrissie was hampered by the costume but managed to kick him with both legs in the stomach, hissing at him to leave her alone. Pagey came at her again. This time Chrissie kicked him on top of Shorter and woke him up.

'I was just trying to find out what exactly was happening.' Pagey was unapologetic. Chrissie realised that she had broken another illusion. She had fought with her shadows and won, which meant that they weren't shadows at all. She glazed over again and sat unblinking, but the magical possibility of escape into something better had gone. Shorter took Pagey by the arm away from Chrissie's side. Chrissie sat upright in the half dark like the sphinx in moonlight, straining for what he said.

'Don't you think, that if she really is the cause of all our misfortune, you should show her some respect?'

'You're right, she's got the power,' said Pagey. They both looked back at her. In the big window, Mars was looming reddish pink, larger and larger till it finally disappeared underneath them and the gassy vastness of Jupiter approached.

'We'll be dead if we go out much further from Mars. We don't have the resources to go back.' As Jupiter grew larger and larger, Shorter thought idly of the telescope his father had bought for him when he was small, in which he had never managed to trap any of these huge bodies. Beyond Jupiter, the sun itself would start to look like not much more than another bright star. Already the sunlight had the tired brown quality of a restless dream. Easey snorted and turned over on his toolbox.

'What do you think she wants *respect* for? I don't think much of the trip so far.' ZV-3 headed straight for the rings of Saturn, then just as it looked as though they were going to collide with one of them, a sheet of slowly moving cosmic debris that would have snuffed them out and added them to its mysterious rotation, they were through it and out the other side.

'I don't know what she wants respect for, I've got a lot of other things on my mind,' Shorter said. 'Take Easey now. This is hardly the right trip to break Easey in is it?' The engineers completed their training by making an external examination of the hull in space. Easey would probably go outside and then forget who he was again. The boy was simple. Pagey said he understood the problem but when the time came he would be sure to help Shorter give Easey his baptism of fire.

Uranus slid by, big and bluey-grey.

'Now there's a planet for you. The old night sky himself, the flash of genius, my planet, Superspeed!' Pagey spoke loudly for Chrissie's benefit, but *The Fair Viol* still continued on its bullet-like course. 'I tell you, I wouldn't have minded stopping there,' Pagey added as the planet moved astern. At this rate they would soon be out of the solar system.

In the same fashion they passed by Pluto, whose eccentric orbit lies inside Neptune's some of the time, making Neptune the outermost planet of the solar system. The light was rapidly worsening and Shorter and Pagey peered out glumly as Neptune hove under the ship.

'I only hope she knows that this is absolutely the last planet in the solar system,' Shorter said quietly.

Then the ship seemed to stand on its nose and point straight down at Neptune. It grew bigger and bigger in the window until it was all they could see, a dull dark wrinkled mass like the hide of a badly lit elephant. Pagey screamed at Chrissie, telling her to slow down, damn you, and in spite of Shorter's warning gestures something seemed to work.

ZV-3 rolled over twice and then pulled up until they were nagivating parallel to the surface of the planet, without disturbing Chrissie's frozen calm, Easey's snoring or Betty's more discreet sleep. Pagey nodded and winked to Shorter. They went in closer and closer until, as neatly as a swallow skims the ground on a rainy day, they had somehow been brought down to ten thousand feet.

'Very nicely done, everyone,' said Shorter, not sure who to praise. The controls were still locked solid, but the instruments said that the ship was flying at two hundred and fifty knots in an atmosphere of four parts nitrogen to one part oxygen, with a ground temperature of fifty degrees Fahrenheit.

Betty woke up. She was feeling marvellous, she said, but she'd die if she didn't have a cigarette. The cushion of air round the ship curiously seemed to make things quieter. Then Easey woke as well in the silence, and gazed out at the wrinkled, dusty planet.

'Are you going to throw me out? Please don't throw me out. It's not me who has brought you here.' All they wanted him to do was his duty, Shorter said. Nobody was under suspicion so far for anything, and if anyone was causing the flight to seem strange, that wasn't a sign for panic, as long as that person was still on board. You don't go and crash yourself, said Shorter loudly, right next to Chrissie's ear, not if you want to live. Chrissie showed no sign of having heard.

Then suddenly there was a noise as if someone was hitting the metal hull of ZV-3 with a hammer very hard. Blows rained down and the whole of the airframe shook. Pagey screamed, 'Flak, boys, flak!' Shorter shook Chrissie and repeated his last sentence. Pagey screamed, 'Come on you mad fuckers, I'm ready for you,' and sat on his titanium-chip combat hat so that his privates would be protected. The noise of giant hammering continued on and off, but only Pagey was in a position to do anything about an attack, and he could see nothing.

Finally, as predicted by Easey, the big round Astroplex in the nose began to come loose. Without any more warning, the whole of the nose-window assembly was lifted off by the slipstream and swung round on the outside of the fuselage, held on by a single bolt. A great wind blew in through the hole, and another noise came in, a deep roar. Climbing up towards the hole with difficulty against the slipstream to inspect the damage, Shorter pulled himself to the lip of the window and peered out.

As he did so, the whole of the ground beneath him became lit up and from horizon to horizon became one vast burning city. At ten thousand feet, Shorter could feel the heat on his cheek. They were in an air raid with planes droning all round, and looking round the sky, Shorter was able to see every type of warplane from the old, old days. Lancasters, Liberators, Wellingtons, Stukas, Heinkels and Messerschmitts, and above them, Halifaxes, Flying Fort-resses, Mosquitoes, as if they had unburied all the heroic anger to fly one last joint sortie, turning block after block of the endless city into a firestorm. It sucked the few survivors off the street into the roaring façades. There was nothing between fire and ice in Chrissie's heart, and this was the fire.

Shorter went back down. Then he and Pagey forced Easey to go outside, to break him in. Easey, praying furiously that all this would be subdued below the event threshold, was pushed out on a rope and managed to put the glass back on and seal it on the outside. This cut down the noise, and by the time he had got back inside the fires were dying away, turning from red to blue and only surviving in patches, like brandy burning out on a Christmas cake. Easey was terrified all the same, out on the fuselage, and only managed to hold himself from going to pieces completely and losing his bowel control and quite possibly his mind again, by repeating to himself that he was doing it for love. Wrestling with the airflow and two types of epoxy resin on the nose, Easey was granted the insight that what he loved (the Mermaid) and what he feared (the spectacle of Armageddon) both had their origins in the same mind, and the knowledge was almost too painful for him to bear. But finally he decided on life and began to inch his way back inside.

Betty was rather good at drawing people out, she thought, and while Pagey and Shorter were holding on to a rope with Easey outside in the airlock, passing him up wrenches and things, she thought it would be a good time to start talking to Chrissie.

'Has the cat got your tongue then?' she enquired after a long silence.

'It's not my fault, what's happening,' Chrissie replied.

'If you wanted to be anything, anything at all, what would you be?'

Chrissie replied, 'A *shark*.'

Betty said, yes, they were graceful creatures, much abused by the motion picture industry, and what on earth was it like in cryo?

'I didn't want to come out. It's like . . . *nothing*. It's nice. It's quiet.'

Shorter and Pagey came in carrying Easey, who looked the same shade of grey as the planet. Betty said, alarmed, 'Has he been shot?' But Shorter said, no, it was a touch of fear, took the use of his legs away.

The light of the firestorm died completely and the cabin went back to combat lighting, rich blue with inky shadows. The hammering noise had recurred intermittently but it was getting muffled, as if there now was a layer of tripe between the two surfaces and the hammer was getting tired punching through it.

Shorter told them about what he'd seen outside. Easey, who had seen it too, nodded dully, as if he'd just had electro-convulsive therapy and was being asked if he was feeling all right.

'And there was flak bursting dead level a hundred yards to port. But I couldn't see anywhere where we'd been hit. I could probably tell for certain if I was flying.' Pagey told Shorter to try again. The joystick still felt as if it was rooted in frozen suet, but Shorter kept working at it patiently and soon declared he had an inch or so of

76

play, and if it opened up any wider it would key the automatic hydraulics in and the old *Fur Vile* would have to answer to his hand. The joystick was a stubby black handle with a gun button on top (not in use on this model) and XONTROL printed round the worn rubber where it came out of the *dash*, as Punting used to insist on calling the console. Pagey knew the *dash*board used to sit in the old petrol cars, so that the passengers had something between them and a smelly filthy engine, and Punting drove the ZV-3 exactly as if it was his sports car, to everyone's alarm. But nobody except Easey called the joystick *Xontrol*.

Betty smiled her most winning smile at Chrissie, and did the introductions to the crew. Boys, this is Christine. This is Gunner E. Page, known as Pagey, and the second pilot, Sergeant R. Short, known as Shorter, or Shortarse said Pagey helpfully.

'And this is our flight engineer. He's called . . .' Betty couldn't see Easey's name tag because he was still recovering on the floor. Finally, as if giving his last will and testament, he breathed out John Brinkley Easey. 'John Brinkley Easey, and he's from Dunwich. Where is Dunwich, John?'

'It's in the sea. It's a drowned village,' Easey replied. Betty smiled as if she understood.

'Yes. Well, John's been doing airborne repairs. But I believe it's quite safe because we've been throttled back, going slow.' Shorter nodded as if it was he who'd been driving, taking his pipe out and putting it back to avoid unsettling some temporary bridgework which the stem rested on.

'Is this the future?' Chrissie asked him, seeing as he seemed to be in charge. Shorter was constrained to take his pipe out again. That was a tricky question, no two ways about it.

'Did you have your heart set on any particular part of the future?' Chrissie thought that he looked a bit wary. She couldn't answer the question for fear of looking stupid. She began to feel the anger creaming up in her again, born like a tornado from massive, contradictory movements. The firestorm threatened to start again outside, for a moment. But then Betty said, 'I really like your dress.' And Chrissie, who had watched Betty from the cruel depths of cryo which made windows into all souls, knew she was telling the truth. Betty approved. Betty *understood*.

'I looked at the date on your canister, Chrissie, and it's at least a million years old,' Pagey lied fluently. Chrissie wanted to hear it and didn't notice it was a lie.

'Really? What happened to my civilisation?' This was another poser but Pagey was indeed a son of flashing genius. Looking sincerely at Chrissie he said, 'To tell you the truth, we didn't go back that far at school. Is that what they wore in them days?' he said, pointing to the mermaid costume. There were more muffled explosions outside. They reminded Pagey of the time he'd been standing on a street corner and watched cars driving over a lot of cans of beer which had fallen off a lorry.

Chrissie looked worried and the ship started to jolt and yaw a little. Suddenly her ears popped. Quickly she said, 'I don't want to go to Neptune, I want to go home.'

Pagey smiled reassuringly. 'We'll see what we can do, princess.'

Then Betty gasped. Standing in the doorway behind Pagey was a ghost.

Captain Punting advanced slowly into the room, which was as fast as his frozen military coat would allow him to move. He was covered in frosting, even on his face and moustache. His eyebrows, ear and nostril hair all had tiny clusters of ice crystals on them, which turned to water in the cabin and made him look as if he was sweating. He was definitely alive. The collected guilt of the crew who had failed to rescue him from his predicament was thick in the air. Punting nodded to the mermaid in Shorter's seat, and leant over her to see where they were. When he'd left they'd been in deep space. But Punting was not thawed out enough for surprise. There was a long pause. They could hear the carbon fibre struts creaking as if the ship were gaining weight. It was, but only Punting so far knew about it.

'You should take her up, number two.' There was no doubt about it. They were sinking towards the surface.

'I've tried,' Shorter said. 'There's not much more I can do at the moment.' But he started working the joystick again, which seemed to have got even more frozen. The surface loomed even closer.

'They'll put you on a charge,' Punting said with great satisfaction. Shorter knew that in the end it was the captain's responsibility. But they'd left him in the hold, which was tantamount to mutiny. Why on earth had he done a stupid thing like that?

'But it's just as well we're going down. I tell you why.' Punting licked his lips unfrozen. 'Hear those explosions? Well, that's cryo canisters exploding. The freezer broke down, it started to get warm, and I was able to free myself, unaided, from a wall of sausagemeat bearing down on me. Every time a can goes off, the ship gets ten stone heavier, so it gets dragged down.'

'Ah, so that's what the noise was.' Pagey sounded relieved, and so Punting turned to try and impress the gravity of the situation on him.

'I know it's just people's lives, Pagey, which don't count for much in the modern generation. But it is your business and the business of the superior officers to try and save life, if possible. Very soon this ship isn't going to be able to sustain flight and it'll drop out of the sky like a brick. So I'm giving the order to abandon ship.' This sounded so wild and strange that Pagey had to laugh.

'Abandon ship? But I've never even *seen* my fucking parachute!'

'It's an order, Gunner Page.' Punting took off his icc-cncrusted coat and pulled a half-length camelhair coat, with a collapsing bowler hat and umbrella, from under the pilot's console. He was now dressed in civvies, as if he had experienced Chrissie's nightmare too, and expected the ground to be thick with the Red Army, the SS, the Home Guard and the Vietcong, all of whom would be ready to cut his throat if they knew he was a pilot.

Pagey went to the locker stencilled PARACHUTES and yanked the handle. Finally it opened with a screech. Inside were three dusty bottles. Now, suddenly, the tables were turned on Punting.

'Very good, Gunner Page. Rescind the order. *I* am going out.' Punting swung his legs over the pilots' console so that his feet were resting on the big glass dome which Easey had so recently repaired. Easey started up to stop him standing on it, but Punting was kicking it and soon had it loose. The airstream carried it round so that it hung by the one bolt on the rim again. The wind noise increased but they couldn't have been doing more than ninety knots. Punting hung with his legs out of the hole, and tapped Shorter lightly on the shoulder with his umbrella before disappearing in the act of unfurling it.

Punting had gone parachuting with an umbrella.

'I hope he kills himself, the cunt,' Pagey said vehemently.

'But what was wrong with the repair I did to the window?' Easey asked. In reply, Pagey pointed to the open door to the hold and the airlock; a long, thick tongue of pinkish-looking material was creeping into the cabin. The hold itself and the way to the airlock would now be completely full.

Pagey and Easey sprang across and managed to slam the door.

80

Pagey said cor, he didn't fancy being fucking drowned in it and Easey laughed.

'Fucking drowned,' he repeated. Pagey looked at Easey. Was the black boy simple or was he taking the piss? He was like a fucking tape-recorder or something.

Then there was a loud dull pop from outside and the urgent wormcast of pink goo which had been squeezing itself round the hinges and through the keyhole stopped pushing. The airlock had now opened under the pressure and ZV-3 flew low across the Neptunian landscape spewing out reconverted matter from its side like a leaking tube of toothpaste. Simultaneously with the pop, Shorter found that the icy grip on the controls slackened and he could move them. He shouted for everyone to get their heads down as he thought he could bring them in. Easey, green as all-get-out, started to panic again about not being able to swim, Neptune being the planet of watery dissolution, but Shorter shouted for him to calm down, that there was no sea visible. It was all woody scrubland, almost desert in the dull light of Neptune's moons. There were dry flashflood channels leading to deeper canyons but no sign of surface water at all.

In the scramble to positions, Pagey managed to flick a piece of the pink sausagey meat on to Chrissie's mermaid tail. She screamed for someone to get the foul thing off her, but then the dry thorny scrubs of Neptune were clawing at the wings and underbelly of ZV-3. Shorter had wisely kept the landing gear up but the ship was way overweight and lashed and crashed and skidded and bumped, finally slithering to a halt at the edge of a sandy wadi. Chrissie stopped screaming and started to whimper about the sausagemeat.

But nobody was listening. Pagey, Betty and Easey by some magic telepathy all spontaneously applauded Shorter. They cheered him loudly. Betty embraced him. Pagey clapped him on the shoulder. Easey touched his forearm. And so it came to pass that Shorter, standing breastplate to breastplate with mortal danger, had outfaced the monster, and brought them safe to land.

Shorter turned round and pushed at a branch which was poking through the nose-cone window. The branch had large mauve leaves on which appeared in deep purple a design of the Eye of Horus. The branch was in the way so Shorter broke it off and threw it outside. The landing lights showed a mean scrub dotted with wiry trees and bushes, all with the same kind of leaves in varying sizes. Shorter said the womenfolk had better stay behind while the menfolk went out to investigate.

Betty was left alone with Chrissie again. Chrissie had the uncomfortable feeling that her breasts were swelling, very much as if she were pregnant. Remembering the night with Ranulph, his excitement, the blood, and her usual rotten luck, she guessed that she was. However she hadn't apparently exchanged any visible characteristics with the tiny phantom beginning to assemble inside her uterine cavity. It was dead unfair. Just because her father's blood had been splashing all around she'd got frightened and Ranulph had got excited and this had been enough to yoke their chemistries together so that she became against her better will and judgement pregnant. Betty removed the sausagemeat but Chrissie still felt sick, and Betty confirmed it was the morning. Chrissie had morning sickness. Betty said comfortably that she was sure there was something they could do about it, and if not why worry? Chrissie said that she'd rather die than have the kid, at her age. Of course it was different when you got to Betty's age. Besides, Betty was attractive and could probably go out with any man she chose.

Betty laughed and pointed outside to where the three men were talking in the half-light of the stars.

'What, *that* lot?' she said, and laughed. She'd had to do with Pagey but he'd taken too much speed and fried his brain, and what kind of a relationship was that? Chrissie said that Ranulph who'd done her old man in had used to mix cow tranks and speed to get

82

the right combination for reality, but she was like Betty, she didn't like to take drugs either. Life was bad enough as it was. Betty hadn't heard the cryo song, 'Life, Love it or Leave it For a While', she said; except for going to work when it was unavoidable she didn't listen much to the music, and liked to spend her time reading or asleep.

Chrissie, hungry to idealise her newfound sister, imagined her stylishly curled up with a picture novel on an oval bed with a white fur counterpane. In fact Betty lived with two other girls who she didn't really get on with. They had beds in the same room in the heart of great, handmade London, just across the river from Chrissie.

'It's handy for Victoria, but I don't really like it there.'

Betty looked out at the three men standing in a group talking. Pagey was smoking. Shorter was pointing with his pipe. Easey was standing too close to them both, and they kept moving away. Behind them the planet seemed uniformly barren. Neptune offered nothing.

'I'm not supposed to tell you this but we're not really a million years in the future.'

'Not even a little bit?' Chrissie asked. Betty said it was a very little bit, but then every little bit made a difference when you put it between yourself and your past miseries. Chrissie thought about that.

'I had this bastard Xontroller who tried to stop me going. Just imagine it. He was trying to y'know, bend the law. Still I suppose he's dead now, even if it is a very little bit of a million years.'

Betty agreed it was quite possible he was dead. She was surprised that they let Chrissie on if she was pregnant, though. How far gone was she when she went in? It was the night before, Chrissie sniffed, he raped me after he killed my dad. She went to Gatwick good and early but the medical was a *joke*, she said.

The men came back in. The world outside was so desolate that Pagey had to go off on a joke tag just to stop himself getting The Fear, and running in concentric circles round and round inside his partly devastated head.

'Hello campers! Good mornin' an' welcome to Butlin's! This is your Redcoat speaking. Before we have the knobbly knees competition, we need volunteers to hack a takeoff strip outa virgin scrub, and scrape 'uman remains out of the freighter.'

'Chrissie's pregnant,' Betty said.

'Ah, very good, change details. Volunteers needed to scrape 'uman beginnings off of Chrissie's insides. What about you, Easey, you look like a man of great surgical potential. I'd take him up on it, Chrissie, it's a very bad part of the universe to get pregnant.'

Chrissie stared at Pagey so balefully that Betty almost expected a bull to come out of the half dark, tuck a horn under his belt and take him off to trample him quietly to death. But nothing happened. Easey asked what was so bad about it.

'Well for a start, there's no hot water. I'd hit the "abort" button if I were you, Chrissie.' Chrissie said acidly that not all girls had 'abort' buttons. Pagey said that anyway it got her off sausagemeat detail. Betty volunteered to go with Pagey to make a start and to get him off Chrissie's back. She pulled him out of the door while he was still making jokes, saying, 'What's the worst job you ever 'ad?'

Outside the stuffy cabin the air was wonderfully cool and fresh. Betty said it was like wine, and Pagey, who never touched a drop, said yeah, like wine. Human debris lay caught up in the low trees and thorny bushes tracing the landing path of the ship. ZV-3 lay tilted on one stubby black wing looking, with its pilot's window hanging half off, like a wounded June bug. Considering the amount of person spread over the landscape, it smelt sweet too. Repelled and fascinated, Pagey reached out and touched a piece.

It was drier than he expected, fibrous and doughy. He rolled a piece between finger and thumb. Whatever you did it wouldn't stick to your hand. The rear of ZV-3 was coated with it; it had poured out of the airlock and the slipstream had rolled it back along the fuselage where it clung in rippling wads, like cooling lava. Pagey ran up the flow to stand on the fuselage of the ship. It felt quite spongy underfoot as if it had already decided to set. He looked down at Betty, who was bending to examine it as well, and wondered if there was time for a sneaky fuck. You could actually do it on the people, as it were. But he knew it would take for ever to argue Betty round, she'd been so off him recently. He sat down on top of the mound and pulled a piece off, and started absent-mindedly rolling it into a ball.

Inside the ship Shorter tried the motors one by one. They were still dead. It would be a pity if they never got back because with Punting gone he'd be sure to be captain. He could just see the expression on the wife's face. He gazed out forward at the dry, ghostly landscape, and wondered if this corresponded with the topography described for the planet in *The Reader's Digest Encyclopaedia of Space*. Then he remembered that the last week's instalment had only been up to 'K'. He'd have to wait a couple of issues to see what they said about it all. A pity there wasn't enough light for a photograph. He liked to take pictures of eclipses with his Instamatic, and the flight path back often lay in the shadow of the earth or moon. He always put the latest ones up over the twin-bar electric heater in the fireplace, below the hologram. Tretchikoff's Green Woman had more sincerity and depth, and used less electricity than the earlier conversation piece, a laser-simulated Mona Lisa with push-button, remote control smile booster.

Well, anyway here they were. Gravity was normal, temperature was normal. Easey's figure walked into the mercury vapour glare of the landing lights. The poor boy looked as if he was moping or lost. Cynthia, who was Shorter's grown-up daughter, had gone through a phase which had caused her parents a lot of anguish, when she'd had a dark-skinned boyfriend. Fortunately his parents had sent him to work for an uncle in Bradford and Cynthia had married someone else. Cynthia was a hairdresser, and lived close to her parents still. Apart from that little brush over Mohammed, they'd been pretty close. Cynthia would have never gone for a Cryo. She had too much going for her, too much self respect. Shorter turned to Chrissie. 'You remind me of my daughter.'

Chrissie stiffened visibly. 'I'd better watch out then.'

It was obviously the wrong remark. Teenagers were so touchy. He should show that he was only trying to be friendly. 'Why did you want to be a mermaid then?'

'To lure ships to their doom,' Chrissie replied.

Outside, Easey who had made a perfect target stumbling slowly about in the ship's landing lights, suddenly fell down. Pagey had made a little stack of doughy missiles and piled them in a pyramid like cannonballs, and was throwing them at everything in range. Easey had been hit in the face with the remains of two elderly sisters from Dorking in Surrey, who had gone for Cryos because they'd become too arthritic to exercise their dogs and that had finally broken their hearts. They'd also illicitly smuggled one poodle in with them, and now they were all one flesh. Easey put his hands up to surrender, but Pagey had got his range and kept throwing. Easey stayed in the light to argue that it was unfair. To stop Pagey being so beastly, Betty crept up behind him and put a little bit of the stuff down his neck. Inside the ship, Chrissie said to Shorter, 'You know I'm controlling all this?' She slid a foot out of her mermaid costume and leant forward to take Betty's nail varnish. 'Betty won't mind if I use this, will she?'

'She won't get a chance, will she, not if you're controlling her.' Shorter thought that Chrissie should know a few things at least about things which had happened before. 'This isn't all you, you know. I'll give you an example. The rest of my life, you don't know anything about, how could you?'

Deep inside Chrissie the worm turned in its sleep, and whispered, 'But I do!'

'I've been forty years in the service. It's not perfect. I've fought for better conditions in the union. Mostly, we've lost. I doubt if you'd understand responsible trades union negotiation and the time and trouble that goes into it. The struggles that we went through in order to have a union at all. If you don't have a union, it's very simple. It means you don't control your own destiny. But as you haven't had any work experience, how could you know about being in a union, young miss?'

'I don't give a toss about your union. We're not in your union now.' Outside, Easey had covered his head and was kneeling. Pagey was using him as a target for slow, mortar-like lobs. Easey hadn't moved out of the light. 'You can think what you like,' said Chrissie, 'but it won't change anything. I'm in charge.'

'So what am I doing here if none of anything I've done is of any consequence to you?'

Chrissie shrugged. 'I can't explain it. But it's the truth.' Shorter thought this was an exceptionally offensive young woman and if he'd been her father he would have liked to have given her a good hiding long ago to stop all this nonsense.

'All right, princess, if you're in charge, how come you got pregnant?'

'That was before. I got pregnant before I controlled everything.'

'So what are you going to do about it now?'

'I'm going to get rid of it.'

There was suddenly the sound of somebody imitating a two-tone door chime outside the airlock. It could only be one person, and he should be dead. For a moment, even Chrissie looked surprised.

'Ping-pong! Ping-pong!' went Punting. 'Hellooo? Any-one-at-ho-wome?' Punting stepped in brightly, and Chrissie felt a wave of anger that he hadn't been killed. It wasn't fair. He looked as if he'd just stepped next door, rather than ratting on the crew as ZV-3 was about to crash-land. Even Shorter was taken aback, and silently lodged his dreams of captaincy. He should have known better. Punting had a genius for survival if nothing else.

'Did you know my umbrella was *ruined*? It blew completely inside out.' Punting lifted it up to show them, then opened the drawer marked PARACHUTES and put it away. 'How's every-body?'

'Chrissie thinks she's the key to all creation,' Shorter said.

'Ah! Then she must be – *pregnant*!' Punting's archness was if anything worse than his other moods. He wagged his finger roguishly at Chrissie. 'Now now my dear, Solipsism is the disease of youth. It is like acne. Eventually one grows out of it.'

From deep in Cryo, Chrissie remembered in a flash Punting's

life, trailing in colourful ragged trains behind him, but stopping abruptly in front of him, in a way which intimately concerned her. She would happily kill him at this stage, only she couldn't get the earth to swallow him up.

Outside, Easey, in whom the past as well as the future were obliterated, sat down nervously as Pagey threw a huge horse collar of the pink stuff at him, catching him as intended square on the shoulders with his head poking through the middle. The horse collar contained a failed poet whose remains were spiralled around a number of Proles who had all belonged to the same bicycling club. Then the halter broke under its own weight and slipped off.

Chrissie thought the games that they were playing were *disgusting*. She was surprised Betty went along with them. Now Pagey was chasing her round, and Betty's high heels were sticking in the dry, doughy mess. Finally Betty took off her shoes and ran for shelter back to the ship, laughing and breathless. Pagey followed her in and tried to stuff a piece down her blouse. They were both bright-eyed and shrieking like little children. Shorter told them to stop fooling around. Then Easey came in and he had got the pink stuff plastered all over his uniform and stuck on to his frizzy hair. In spite of herself, Chrissie managed a laugh. He looked so stupid. Then Pagey found a joint in his top pocket, lit it and passed it round.

'I don't mind if I do,' said Punting. Chrissie had some but it didn't make her feel much better, although it did make her feel really hungry. She hadn't eaten for ages.

'What's for supper?' said Punting suddenly, rubbing his hands. Betty opened the provisions box. A mess of mildewed bread, used tomato ketchup sachets and half eaten biscuits on wet paper plates stared back at her. Ground crew had been on work to rule, so nothing had been changed. Shorter grunted.

'Looks like we're going to starve, then,' he said. Punting looked round keenly at the crew. His eyes had a merry twinkle.

'Hands up who wishes to die slowly by starvation?' he said.

Chrissie put her hand up. 'Chrissie that's only half a vote, remember you're eating for two.'

'Well, there's no animals here, and no vegetables to speak of,' said Shorter slowly. Shorter didn't really like vegetables. He'd been on a high-grain diet for his angina now for a couple of years to squeeze past the annual medical. He didn't have an 'in' with one of the doctors like Punting, and he missed pork chops, and crackling, and even something the missus did to perfection (though Cynthia said it was vulgar), which was pig's trotters in jelly. And then there were all the other things he couldn't eat now, like blood sausage with its little cubes of diced fat, and there was an Irish butcher's just down from Lavender Hill who made lovely big bangers, six to a pound and they'd squirt fat when you pricked them. The missus told him he'd dig his grave with his teeth if he wasn't careful. And here was Punting about to lay some awful temptation in his way. Shorter watched with interest. Punting was holding up a strand of the pink stuff, with his eyebrows raised, awaiting general approbation.

'For crying out loud,' said Pagey. 'You're making me feel ill.' Punting asked what exactly he had been playing with out there. 'That was just – mucking about. *Eating* it, that's different.'

Easey was crying. Outside he had been an involuntary spy on Pagey, who at one stage had pressed himself up against Betty, while raising her skirt and trying to get close to her with a stick or rod which came out of his flies. Betty had moved away when she'd seen Easey but in the thick fog of Easey's mind he began to feel suspicion that not everybody shared the knowledge that they came from the sea. The fog lifted for a moment and Easey saw a man and a woman lying together naked on the grass, doing what Pagey had wanted to do. They were in a glade. The man withdrew. His stick was drooping and covered in juice. The woman was happy to be with him and he lay in her arms. *So that's how it happens*, thought Easey. It made him feel slightly nauseated. Where then was the sea?

'I think there is one word which frees us from the taboos which we adopt in our civilised society, to prevent us from surviving in this situation,' Punting said. 'The word normalises the situation *vis-à-vis* the remains of our fellow mortals. Now, everybody, what is the word?'

'Toad in the 'ole,' said Pagey. Punting shook his head. 'Toad all over the place.' Punting smiled and wagged his finger. Wrong again. 'Toad in a basket?'

'Close,' said Punting, encouraging Pagey to continue.

'Toad right next to the basket.' Punting thought he'd have to start giving absurdly broad hints. It was sad how education had declined. He said, slowly and deliberately so that everybody could have a chance to guess it right, 'Now what do you do to toad before you eat it?'

Pagey said immediately, 'Catch it, an' wallop it to death.'

'And *then*?' Punting was really getting tired of spoonfeeding the crew. He picked up a piece of the pink stuff off Easey's eyebrow. 'The word, the sacrament we are all looking for, is called – *Cooking*!'

They were going to do it, too. Chrissie closed her eyes and tried to faint. Punting said it was more than a pleasure to eat, it was their duty to stay alive for as long as possible in order to be rescued. The boys went out to gather firewood, and Betty started laying the table.

At the back of the parachute locker Betty found some candle ends and a candleholder which held seven candles in a row. Punting peered at it and declared it to be a bona fide kosher candelabra, a miniature model of the seven heavenly bodies visible to the naked eye. Furthermore it was concrete proof that a lineup of the planets had happened before. Punting served them all from an old mess tin.

'It shows we are not the first,' he said, rewarming it over the candelabra. Chrissie sat aloof. Punting remarked that there was no need for anyone to hold back as there was plenty for everyone. Betty got some music on the radio. Everyone seemed to be having a good time except for Chrissie when suddenly Easey burst into tears. Punting thought it was the food.

'There there, dear boy, don't fret. This is for your own good, you know. We rely on you to repair the ship. Can't have you wasting away.'

'No sir, it's not that. Until recently I have not been well up in my education . . .' Easey stared round, trying to assemble the words to express his grief.

'It's all right, Easey, we don't expect you to keep up with the sparkling dinner-party conversation,' said Pagey. The pink stuff, if it wasn't too lightly cooked, went down rather well, Shorter thought. He wished Pagey would stop getting at Easey though.

'Can't you shut up and just eat?'

Pagey smiled back at Shorter. '*Really* witty conversation, innit. "Shut up an' eat."'

'It's the facts of life,' Easey said. 'I just found out the facts of life.'

Shorter felt sorry for the boy in spite of himself. 'They *are* rather shocking, actually, if you think about them.'

Easey's discovery that men and women came not from the sea proper but from the hot, fish-smelling junction of the sexes suddenly seemed to pass from him and he began to eat. Punting had uncovered a bottle of Taiwanese whisky called 'Glen Glasgow' and was already halfway down the label with it. Nobody else seemed to be drinking much at all. He took one of Shorter's mentholated toothpicks without asking and tilted his chair back. Chrissie watched him with pure hatred from the shadows, willing his chair to tip right back. But as always with Punting, something seemed to save him. Chrissie's belief in her power was waning fast.

'Has anyone dined at the Savoy Grill recently?' Punting shook his head as if he was about to impart sad news. 'Because it's really changed since the old days. Then, you had waiters breaking from the four corners of the room during a banquet at the conclusion of each succulent course. With their white coats on they looked like gulls following a plough.

'Next, in the afternoon sun, a walk down the Strand. Maybe buy a shirt. Full of affection for the human race.'

Shorter looked at his geranium wilting. He loved geraniums. He felt helpless, though. They weren't made for life under combat lighting.

'There's not much sun here. You can hardly pick it out from the rest of the stars.' Punting nodded sadly in agreement and took some more 'Glen Glasgow' in a long series of swallows.

'Feeling better now, Easey?' he enquired, as he put the glass down. The malt-style liquor put a fiery ring around his insides that cut the grease nicely. But that was why the Scots always drank whisky with haggis. Otherwise it would be almost impossible to digest, it was so stiff with tallow. Easey smiled at him, grateful for the interest.

'Yes, thank you sir. It was just that I thought I might be eating someone's —' Easey stifled a retch and began piteously, 'You see, it's what the bits are used for that upsets me. I thought people were born from the sea.'

'Not at all an unreasonable belief,' said Punting. 'Originally, we did all come from the sea. But that was a long time ago. People who think they come from the sea now, or like to pretend they do, are really making complete fools of themselves.'

This was the final straw as far as Chrissie was concerned. She jumped up and turned the main lights on. Everyone was dazzled for a moment. Chrissie adjusted her mermaid costume and snorted loudly.

'Leave it out,' said Pagey.

'Chrissie, *don't*, we're having a party,' Betty said anxiously. She was actually quite enjoying the lights and the music, and the conversation. It was easy to destroy the bubble and make everyone leave.

'You've all been lying to me. All of you. A million years! Like *fuck*! Betty told me! You're a lot of lying bastards!'

Betty stepped outside for a breath of fresh air and Pagey followed her. It had been nice while it lasted, the meal. Easey blew out the candles one by one, after Shorter had lit his pipe off one and gone out for a stroll.

'Poor Chrissie,' said Easey, in complete sincerity. 'It must be hard for her to be stuck out here. We all enjoy each other's company but she would probably rather be watching tv, and on top of that, her father's dead.' There's always someone worse off than you, Easey thought. But there must be something out there on the planet which he could find and give Chrissie, as a sign of his respectful love for her. As long as it didn't lead to anything which made him feel sick. Wiping his mouth with a red paper towel, Easey waddled off purposively into the night.

At the table, Chrissie sat down defiantly opposite Punting and the remains of the 'Glen Glasgow'.

'So! You don't want anyone to love you.' Punting looked at her with rheumy sorrow. 'I wish people loved me. I know they don't, though. Who would you rather be? Mine is an unhappy fate.' Punting drank a little. 'It's not just that I rat on people in tight corners, it's that I survive! Every time, something miraculous happens. I've had my life reeled back in front of my eyes so many times that the film's beginning to get scratched. How I love the good old days! Why on earth d'you *want* to go into the future? It seems to me the golden age is in the past.'

Chrissie said the future was going to be better than the past, definitely, no two ways about it.

'In the future, everybody you know will be dead. I suppose that in your present mood . . .' Punting shrugged. 'I must say, in my wildest binges, I never thought to wake up that late. To put yourself out for a million years . . .' Punting had never talked to a Cryo before, and he was glad of the opportunity of hearing the other side's point of view. He didn't mind shipping them any-where if they were sincere. It was a pity Chrissie had popped out but as soon as they were back on earth she could always pop back in.

'Here's to you, my dear. The best of luck. And I toast the great memory gap, oblivion, the atheists' heaven, the stretch of *nothing*. I do it to myself in a small way. I don't know why it worries me. After all I go to sleep every night. And yet I couldn't go for that length of time. As far as the big one goes, I'm afraid.'

'If it was not for the Cryogenic Programme, there would be too many unemployed for the state to support and our whole way of life would be threatened. Besides creating work for the crews and skilled jobs constructing the freighters and capsules, medical knowledge has also been advanced because of the intensive research into human tolerances of the cryogenic process.' Punting started to laugh and slap his thigh to hear a Cryo quote the government so verbatim. It was almost as good as videobuggery, which Punting had chuckled away whole Saturday afternoons watching.

Chrissie continued: 'The Cryogenic Programme means that you can do something for yourself and something for your country all at the same time and involves no personal expenditure. It does involve technology however and Britain's Cryogenic Programme is the most humane and is technologically leading the field, with the exception of the United States, Russia and the members of the Common Market.' Chrissie looked out of the broken window on to the sad wastes of Neptune, then continued. Punting was nagged by the memory of the Eye of Horus, and stopped listening. He had seen it somewhere before.

'Remember to remove false teeth before passing the bodies into the matter converter,' Chrissie was reciting in a dull voice. 'Those with pacemakers, surgical pins and colostomies are not advised to take part in the programme, nor are those who are pregnant, as the reconversion of matter on termination is not programmed for more than one cell matrix.'

Horus was the Egyptian sun-god. The Egyptians had married astronomy and astrology to economics and theology but it was unlikely that they had got out to Neptune. Chrissie's voice suddenly became low and passionate, as the sound of the crew returning was heard outside.

'And I'm going into the future, because everything that happens now is shitty, and there's no hope, none at all, understand?'

Betty came in pulling Easey after her. He had something in his hands that twinkled and shone and shimmered. Pagey, behind them in the airlock, had somehow got the top half of a dinner-jacket and was wearing it over his sweatshirt and dirty fatigues, with a yellowing fringed silk scarf thrown over the shoulder. Easey had a dinner-jacket on too, extremely elderly and double-breasted, and was wearing a large woollen hat with a bobble on the top. Betty had on a short black coat over her uniform, and was carrying another handbag. Punting looked up quizzically and Betty turned the music off which had been playing on the radio. She tried to get Punting to listen, saying there was music playing outside, good music, but Punting could tell even though he was a mite deaf that something had happened.

'I say! Here I am berating princess here for looking forward to a golden age and it jumps in on us. Are we off to a party? Where on earth did you find it?' Betty took the shimmering thing from Easey and held it up for Chrissie to see. Instantly, Chrissie knew it was *her*, and she couldn't wait to get out of the mermaid costume.

'I bought it for you,' said Easey. 'It's made from silica from the asteroid belt. Space pearls, they said. So it's out of this world.' Betty said, Chrissie's got an admirer.

'He found it in a second-hand shop,' said Pagey. 'We were all just walking along when this bloke popped his head out of the ground, and asked if I wanted a joint. Behind him we could hear all this music. But if you looked behind him, you could see this narrow street all honeycombed with casinos and restaurants and discos and then even deeper in the earth, a flyover with big cars, and these huge advertisements for Gordon's Gin which he said they gave away, all of this under the earth. That's where the people live here.'

Shorter came in wearing a rather nice sleeveless leather jacket with MARTIAN MERCHANT BANKS embossed on the back. It would do very well for gardening. Chrissie was excitedly getting into her asteroid-belt dress while Easey looked away steadfastly out of the window. She hadn't thanked him, but it was enough for him that she was pleased. Even Shorter looked flushed. But something was holding Punting back.

'I don't know if I'm *with-it* enough for discos.'

Pagey said, what about discos with Gordon's Gin? 'Why does that ring a bell?' Punting said.

'I think we could probably get you fixed up in there, Chrissie, with an operation,' said Betty. Chrissie looked worried and said she didn't have any money, but Betty said never mind, something will turn up.

Shorter was rather looking forward to a little excursion. The music was right on the threshold of audibility, and sounded to him like Great Hits from the Age of Swing. Pagey thought it was a straight ripoff of Buddy Holly, and Betty was reminded of Vivaldi. Punting, deaf, and searching in the fog with only the Eye of Horus as a clue, suddenly came across what he was looking for.

'Gordon's Gin and discos. Wait. I have been here before. Oh my God, the worst bits are coming back to me. Oh my God.' Punting watched open-mouthed as the mills of his memory began to grind. He addressed the empty air. 'Did I really do that?' With an effort he pulled himself together, apologising and saying that his self-censoring mechanism had broken down for a moment, and he was sat in judgement on himself. He quickly recovered and addressed the crew.

'Neptune. Yes. It's a terrifying place. Strong drink is free. You only pay for beer. I wouldn't know about anything else, but as a rule of thumb, the worse it is for you, the easier it is to get. I mean drugs. And then they have these hospitals supplying the drugs and people also sell bits of themselves to the hospitals till there's nothing left of them, for transplanting on to millionaires. It's a dreadful place! The most expensive restaurants in the universe. They will cost you an arm and a leg. The houses are made of paper, you can usually hear people being murdered next door.

'When I was here last, a consortium of businessmen had bought up all the public lavatories and were charging around a tenner for a piss. Private houses of all kinds are dangerous. You could stand to lose an organ, or be broken up for spare parts. Murder is punishable by a small on-the-spot fine. Stay in public places or go in twos. As far as recreation . . . Bordellos are safe, but less popular than Mouthys. I'm sure you all know what Mouthys are.' Punting looked around. No one knew.

'I don't want to upset Easey . . . A Mouthy is a cross between a fruit machine and a fantasy sex-life. The aim is to hit the jackpot, and the reward is an electronic simulation of congress.'

Betty whispered to Chrissie that she was sure Chrissie would strike lucky, and to see if they could get into a hospital party. Chrissie nodded. She was ready for anything.

Pagey couldn't believe his ears about the Mouthys. There was that Arab proverb about a woman for pleasure, a boy for delight, and a melon for ecstasy. Three melons in a row must be something almost unimaginable, a true Jackpot.

'Thanks for the info,' he said quietly to Punting. 'See you later.'

Punting suddenly stood up smiling his old, wicked smile. 'It's a pleasure,' he said. 'I'll go too.'

As they went below the surface of Neptune, Easey remembered with slight trepidation his last encounter with a supposedly alien civilisation. Having arrived from the sea and stolen the name of a dead-and-buried Christian, he had wandered up the coast with no more to clothe himself than that. He had found a coin in a Sheringham pleasure arcade and, totally naked, had played the fruit machines there, winning every time and causing a small riot over the piles of money that he left everywhere, for he'd no idea of the use the stuff might have. Furthermore, every time he won, the flesh tassel between his legs swelled and grew big. In twenty minutes, he made a thousand pounds for the citizens of Sheringham, and caused a riot which wrecked the seafront and overturned two steam locomotives.

The Sheringham police were so appalled at the black angel who had descended amongst them that they couldn't decide what to charge him with. In the end, mysteriously, he was simply given a cup of tea and put on a train to London, with the threat of castration, uttered in the softest of Norfolk accents, ringing in his inner ear: '*If we foind yew araound here agen, blackee, we'll cut your tail arf.*'

Though it was far from Norfolk, Easey heard the clash and clatter of the fruit machines and the hoarse shouts of the Mouthy barkers, and decided at all costs he must avoid the pleasure arcades. There was so much to see. He wished Chrissie and Betty wouldn't walk so fast.

Whole space fleets had trodden the steps down into Neptune and simply disappeared. Platoons of space Enforcement had followed and the same thing had happened to them. There was no redress either. It was impossible to contact a genuine ruling body on Neptune. Neptune was a city which occupied the whole of the hollowed-out inside of the planet. It was a giant honeycomb of parishes upon parishes, wards upon wards, cities coiled and twined inexplicably around each other's boundaries as promiscuously as any two lovers who had chosen the same container to be matter-reduced in together.

The city was in constant motion as well, building and demolishing, filling in, excavating, piling and sifting. Neptunians had little use for conventional products. The environment was largely closed with the exception of a few small stairways to the outer crust, and a large hole over the centre of an inner cavern the size of Manhattan, called Millionaire's Park. This meant that the heat of any action was contained, and the temperature was kept constant by heat pumps which constantly poured the heat back into power. Except for the great hospital corporations which traded with them, Neptunians never gave a thought to the invisible stars and planets. The surface of the planet was so neglected that Punting had said there was no need to lock the spacecraft.

Pagey giggled as the urban wind hit him carrying the big-city vibes. A million thrills! A million pill freaks! He tried to work out if it was his numerologically lucky day so he could get it on with a fruit machine. Now he was in the city, it wasn't the sex so much that interested him, it was the winning.

Punting still couldn't hear the music but there was plenty of other stuff to pay attention to. He shouted to the group that he was going to do a binge, and dived off the main thoroughfare into a narrow street hung about with baskets, like a Mediterranean seaside town. But when he looked close, he saw that in each of the baskets there was a mermaid. It was not a true one, but a triumph of microsurgery. The baskets were gently sprayed with a mist of cool water, and a disembodied voice asked Punting to step inside and see more lovable playmates, little huggable mistresses who could never run away, darling, sensual friendly aquatic pets. The larger mermaids mewed piteously and held out their arms to him, the small ones seemed apathetic, or asleep.

The one real mermaid had been grown from a clone tank, but was ugly. It was true they could never run away on Neptune. The rivers spiralled down towards the interior and never reached any sea. Instead they poured on to the stainless-steel cover of the huge, hot, hundred-mile diameter stone at the heart of the planet, and were turned to steam which drove turbines to pump them laboriously up to the surface again.

Punting was about to go when he saw Easey staring at the mermaids, hypnotised by the sweet-talking shop pavement. Punting led him away by the elbow. The boy was going to need some guidance, to say the least.

'Don't get trapped into any spare-part surgery racket. If you get in a tight corner, show them your space badge. They're not supposed to cut anything off non-residents.' Punting clapped him on the shoulder and strode off. He'd left Easey standing outside the stern, grey, mock-Parisian façade of a brothel. At least the boy would be safe there for a couple of hours. Easey watched Punting's figure limping jauntily till suddenly it was gone, and he became aware that the pavement had surrounded him with rings of deliciously coloured light, and was sending a current of static up his legs to awaken his tassel. Come, the door murmured in three hundred and sixty languages, come. Easey looked up at the twelve lit windows with their red curtains, and began to move towards the door. Punting had said that it was safe. Unfortunately he had forgotten to tell Easey how much safety cost, and Easey, not having any, had not brought any money.

Within half an hour, Betty had found Chrissie a hospital party, which was being held in an empty multi-storey carpark. The flagellants, the mutants, the necrophiliac monsters and the merely curious all came to the parties to see the surgeons bid against each other in Dutch auctions for young limbs still attached to bodies. Those with part or all of their body for sale walked on makeshift platforms, with the part exposed, or in the case of internal organs, a hole cut in the clothes and the part outlined on the skin in fluorescent ink. There were visible-light and ultrasonic scanners on the auctioneers who batted their lids and strutted under the keen and informed gaze of a large crowd. Pretty nurses circulated with trays of drugs, and as always on Neptune, the music was there, pulsing under the skin of the event, keying the frequency-triggered lights in the floor and the low ceiling. In the middle of the crowd, a Mood Maid stood, pumping out further Good Vibes, from its concave sides.

Chrissie and Betty caught the lift to the top of the carpark and stepped out on to the roof. It was, as always in Neptune, a warm night and the Mood Maid could be felt with the music even through the concrete floor. Chrissie threw her handbag down and danced to the music while Betty looked on admiringly: Chrissie was going to be lost to the world and now look at her, bubbling with life. The asteroid-belt dress was a bit old-fashioned with its off-the-shoulder look and hemline below the knee, but as Chrissie danced she looked better and better in it. Betty felt her eyes prickling with tears of happiness for the girl.

Then a surgeon had come up to Chrissie and asked her to dance. He was tall, grey-haired and distinguished-looking, with a tight-fitting, one-piece operating suit on. Chrissie, springing round her handbag, said she was already dancing, thank you, but the surgeon meant downstairs where the scanners kept panning the crowd as if they were looking for shoplifters in a supermarket.

So they went downstairs again for a bit and both danced with the surgeon who suddenly left them to talk to the floppy-jockey who picked the video disks for the synched 3D mobile abstracts and ran the cameras and suddenly there was this gorgeous wave of sound for them and all the scans were pointing in their direction. Chrissie danced like a maniac, gathering an admiring circle of mutants, but Betty felt slightly nauseated and had strange tickling feelings inside her as the scanners probed her inner organs politely but at God knows what frequency. There was so much natural excitement surrounding Chrissie that the self-regulating Mood Maid almost turned itself off. The scanners recorded both of them in their entirety to twelve digits including temperature and radiation readings and stored all the data in the hospital's memory banks digital miles beneath their feet, so that they could be eidetically remembered:

> *Superprole! We treasure your hologram,*
> *And kiss your memory lane!*

The surgeon returned, bringing an anti-noise with him so they could talk. The androgyne go-go dancers from Jupiter slowed down around them as the noise was killed and moved their strokable, muscular but shapely limbs elsewhere. 'Good boys,' the surgeon murmured as the Ganymedes drifted away. Chrissie thought they looked quite nice in unisex leather and chiffon but no one of any status would be seen with a Ganymede as their romance circuitry was so limited. The hospitals imported them, the surgeon explained. Naturally, it was illegal. One of the last acts of the old central authority before its complete collapse had been the banning of trade with other planets. But the surgeon said to the girls that he could wink at the fact that they were from Earth, but he would like them to understand what they were getting into.

The character of Neptune had only begun to emerge as the cities dug deeper and deeper and finally merged into one. There sprang up bloody gang wars where in countless waves of paranoia and delusion ectomorph and endomorph were inspired by unidentified spiritual leaders to mutual mass murder in pitched battles deep in the hot interior. The dead were only measurable by the cubic mile. Law and order ceased, and the hospitals, professionally uninvolved and suppliers to all the surviving wounded, came to power. Thousands of years later, the hospitals still remained the only force for good, the surgeon explained, but there was no way they could collect revenue except by turning Neptune into a free-trade zone. In the name of free enterprise, he bid them welcome.

'Local currency is the *Aitch*. An arm or a leg is one *Aitch*. Internal organs rather more. A kidney, we'd give you three *Aitch*. A lung, $H4.5$. Hysterectomy $H5.8$. Cardiovascular is being renegotiated with the Patients' Union. In addition to payment, we guarantee, should you wish it, to replace the missing organ with a genuine working replica.' Chrissie had noticed at the party that half the people there had something missing. With the feeling they might be getting in too deep, she said, 'But we don't have any money.'

'No no, of course not. *We* pay you! It's the millionaires here you see who set the market going because they use up organs the whole time. It started when the coke people discovered they could throw away their old nose and get another one, and it spread from there. Some people sell their whole bodies, but even with our technology, there's still something about plastic people that's not right. There's a high suicide rate where you've got everything manmade except the brain. We can't buy and sell brains, of course that would be slavery.

'We're a little worried on the hospital board by the current fashion which is towards *nothing*.' The surgeon almost spat the word out. 'People who don't bother to replace organs with adequate working replicas think it's somehow a fashionable comment on society to go around with fewer and fewer organs and then they will die because everyone needs a spleen, and by the time we get to them the rest of them will have probably decayed so we won't be able to use that either.

'*Nothing* is the relic of the old Neptunian spirit which we've tried so hard to stamp out. It's a sort of perverted, self-destructive aestheticism. It is probably incomprehensible to outsiders, but the impulse stems from an overactive imagination. For instance; what is more beautiful than your earthly Venus de Milo? Has she not got lovely arms? Do you not admire her perfectly shaped hands? Continue that trend into society where people make works of art of themselves, and then if you sport a little bit of *nothing*, it shows you know what Art is. Art is *nothing*.' The surgeon stared at the Mood Maid's thread-thin laser beam which reached out into the semi dark above Millionaire's Park to make contact with the hovering auto-debit meter. Maids were an expensive way of making the party swing.

'Fortunately, the move to *nothing* hasn't caught on yet amongst the millionaires. Otherwise, the whole economy would collapse.' Betty said that if people were so bored that they were chopping bits off themselves to pass the time, why didn't they try cryogenics? The surgeon said that cryo used to be the answer, but the re-entry problems were never satisfactorily solved and when people did make it back, they usually arrived to the same set of problems they had left. Chrissie asked how much the surgeon would pay for a termination. The surgeon's eyebrows shot up.

'A hundred *Aitch*, if you're interested. But you won't be around to collect it, because we're obliged to kill the brain. You'd have to nominate your benefactors.'

'I don't mean me, I mean terminate a pregnancy.'

'Of course, how stupid of me, I overlooked it on the scan. Did you come all this way just to sell it?'

Chrissie mumbled that no she hadn't, and she didn't know exactly how she got pregnant either but on earth they were a bit behind on that kind of thing. The surgeon suddenly excused himself and went to a meeting of white-coated figures in a corner who were bargaining with a voluble, attractive dark-haired girl sporting three pairs of arms and a sari; the goddess Siva. He'd taken the anti-noise with him too and the Ganymedes drifted back, weaving in the shock of the renewed music all together, like sea kelp in a heavy surf. Chrissie felt crowded, and fought her way to the concrete ledge for some air.

Betty really was a good sort. She followed Chrissie, hugged her tight and said it would all be all right. They went up to the top of the building again away from the music, where the lift opened on to a small park. The grass was thick with prone amputees on their way to *nothing*, but it was quiet apart from their snores and groans. Even the fountain worked, spitting out rusty water, and Chrissie wetted her temples and wrists and felt better. The pigeons dozed uneasily in rows on the ventilator stacks and as Betty looked, the banks of floodlights began to snap on one by one in a simulated sunrise over Millionaire's Park.

The lift also served the hospital and every so often the doors would open and a body would fall or walk out, sometimes with a paper operating-gown still on. With the dawn, most of them woke and moved away.

A pair of Ganymedes came up in the lift and stumbled out of it together, making love. They were not supposed to respond to each other, but they were both misprogrammed. They fucked noisily and convincingly, their slim, multi-jointed pricks diving round each other like snakes and occasionally diving past to home briefly in a burrow. They lay down together on the parapet, making a noise together like seagulls fighting.

One of the amputees was still trying to sleep. Irritated by the noise, he inched himself over to the robots and without warning pushed them over the edge.

Forty floors down the Ganymedes were starting to scrape against the wall of the building, which sloped gently outwards, and their misdirected spasm continued in a shower of sparks as their plastic flesh ablated, revealing the metal underneath. Chrissie watched as the shooting star became fainter and disappeared in the thick haze a mile below. The ragged pigeons stepped off the night's perch and flew off glumly. Then a black figure stumbled out of the lift, with a silver bandage round its head above the ears, clutching a woolly bobble hat and wearing a spacefreighter badge. It also had a large behind. It was Easey.

Betty and Chrissie sat him up but he had no control over anything at first. He was like a rag doll. Then slowly his eyes centred, and the rest of him followed suit. As soon as he looked as if he could speak, Betty asked him, did you have an accident, Easey? A strange expression came over his face and settled there.

'I'm not Easey,' he said. 'Have you got a mirror?' Betty passed him one and he looked at himself in the mirror. 'Yes, that's him,' he said. Then he dropped the mirror and it broke on the concrete. 'Sorry, it takes some time getting used to someone else's body,' he said. Easey had acquired an accent and said '*tarm*' for time. The old Easey had modelled himself on the first people he spoke with, the Norfolk Constabulary, and had said '*toy-im*'.

'You mean you're not Easey? If you're not from ZV-3, what are you, a clone?' The man who was not Easey rolled his eyes a touch like the old Easey, but it was clear it wasn't Easey.

'Easey's dead. He died in my body. He couldn't work the traffic out. He got squashed by a convoy of robot trucks. Medical writeoff, even here. He should have looked out. This is an all-real body though, I can feel it. No plastic . . . nice. Only trouble is, it's a bit fishy and cold.'

Chrissie was close to tears with anxiety about the operation and wished Not-Easey would go away. He had a ghost of an inflection to Easey's carriage when he walked; the substitution had got her all confused. She looked out over the edge where the Ganymedes had fallen and frightened herself into thinking she was going to fall too. Then she sat down. The fear had connected her for a moment to the indifferent, cryogenic visionary sleep where the past and future are all one, and she remembered Easey had walked from one mist into another. But she still didn't know if Not-Easey was telling the truth. There was something funny about him.

The funny thing about Not-Easey was that he'd been a woman, up to the point he met Easey. He had given Easey 'deep massage' in the brothel, only to find Easey had no money. The (then) woman, cursing herself for being so trusting, had demanded of the bewildered Easey that he go and peddle his enormous behind so he could pay for his out-front pleasure. But Easey was so gawky and gauche and unfamiliar that the woman, who was a weekend body jumper anyway, said she'd let him off if she could use his body, which intriguingly had no plastic, for a few hours. Easey had agreed and they had swapped brains in a street-surgeon's booth. The woman had felt strange in the large, unfamiliar body whose volume of seed had earlier made her gag, but she was stuck with it. Her body, and Easey's brain, were now a long sticky bump in the Equatorial Freeway Automatic Fast Lane, squeezed into a fast-drying streak in the ecliptic by the big rubber wheels of the robot trucks.

Every time a body fell out of the lift, Chrissie would jump, thinking it was the surgeon come back for her. Betty had been down once. The party was over but she had talked to one of the nurses who had promised to remind the surgeon about Chrissie as soon as his meeting was over. Chrissie wanted to run away but stayed, biting her nails. Betty said not to worry, thinking that if it all worked out Chrissie would never want to go back to cryo. Chrissie walked up and down the path next to the parapet, clenching and unclenching her hands.

Easey had been in love with Chrissie and now another brain sat in his body watching her walk up and down. Body jumping with another sex, provided they were healthy, was always a rush. Like someone in a new car, Not-Easey thrilled to the feel of Easey's body with its calm animal strength, and allowed the masculinity, as unmistakable as boar taint, to come riding in on his blood through the arteries to the brain so deftly transposed by the street surgeon.

Not-Easey looked at Chrissie's trim ankles and taut little buttocks as they strutted, and directly valves opened at the base of his tassel and the salty blood poured into the erectile tissue. Each little sac filled out with the flood tide as taut as a spinnaker and the edifice rose. Not-Easey gazed at Chrissie's nipples as they rode at anchor under the twinkling dress, and sperm production rocketed, in frank anticipation of shortly loosing off another batch of tiny frogmen. Not-Easey became suffused with lust. Even Chrissie's edgy desperation was understood as a kind of come-on, a pert alertness. Not-Easey staggered to the parapet and looked down to avoid looking at Chrissie, leaning far over the edge with his new, unfamiliar body. He almost toppled over, but pulled himself back.

Alarmed, he lay on the parapet and hung on for dear life, scarcely daring to breathe.

Sensing the closeness of death and an embrace, albeit to concrete, Easey's ganglions clubbed together for one final effort. As he lay on the parapet, Not-Easey was suffused with the most fabulous orgasm, which began at the tips of his toes and when it ebbed left his head and heart shaken with the closeness to the fires of creation. Not-Easey raised his head finally, to see a different being standing racked with nerves in the asteroid-belt dress. It was just a girl.

'Can I do anything to help?' he said. Betty said no, that they were just waiting, happy to do nothing. Not-Easey said that he used to do nothing once. But he meant a Neptunian *nothing*, and he expected earthly *nothings* to be different. *Nothing* on Neptune was hard, and its aesthetics often involved mutilation.

'We're waiting to hear if Chrissie can have an abortion,' said Betty. 'Excuse me, but if you aren't Easey, who are you?'

Not-Easey wasn't sure yet who he was. A body was like a house you never left, and his old body was now mostly a flaky crust which the robot trucks were turning to powder.

'I did *nothing*, but before that I used to play the Mouthies. I should explain I was a woman.' Neither of the girls blinked. 'I had a system and I won on it. I used to get these orgasms which went on for hours. In the end the Mouthy owners got stroppy and claimed I was draining electricity out of the grid, so that the Mouthies lost money. They warned me off. There was one legless one who caught me one day and he cut my arms off, so that I lost my touch. Whatever they say about plastic, it's not the same.' Not-Easey flexed his fingers. 'I could get my revenge, now.' Chrissie asked him what exactly was involved in a Neptunian *nothing*. Not-Easey smiled the indulgent smile of one who has had access to mysteries so arcane that they can only be approached by oblique parables, and for her he spoke the parable of his life.

'Well, nothing meant I worked as little as possible. Once a month I'd go to the whorehouse to turn tricks for my rent, that was where I met Easey. But the rest of the time I could get by without money. I had a friend who worked in a hospital incinerator who slipped me the odd parcel, so I didn't have to worry about restaurants.

'And my room was empty, except of dust. An empty room is more full of *nothing*. Afternoons I would spend down by the river, when I got up. Occasionally I would be picked up by a millionaire but I would never go to their place. I was not, understand, ready for annihilation. But it was at the river that I could feel *nothing*. Sometimes, when it was neither high nor low, when one boat had gone and another not yet come, and there were no corpses, and the wind blew uniformly low, then I was able to approach the essence of *nothing*. Only the orgasm can be compared to *nothing*. And how long does that last normally, fumbled at by some millionaire in a dusty room?' Not-Easey saw they weren't listening.

Chrissie suddenly saw the surgeon approaching. Her heart almost missed a beat.

'Excuse me,' Not-Easey said. 'I must get to *work*.' He walked into the lift and the doors closed. The surgeon nodded to Betty, smiled at Chrissie and spoke.

'I'm afraid that we can't offer you a termination without the consent of the terminee.'

Neptunians had enormous facility for hypnosis, auto-suggestion and something quite horrid called Eidetic Primal Recall, or what it was like being an unfertilised egg and at the same time being a number of eager sperm who'd made it up the tail-race and were trying to break back into the circle of being. The stress and competition of the moment was the root cause of many of the distresses and delusions of later life, and the Neptunians could never agree on where life began, as they had so much information on its origins. There were killings, road accidents, suicides and murders a-plenty on Neptune, but since no one was really in charge these did not weigh on anyone's conscience. That war had no front line, but there was no doubt that had the surgeons hauled in a medium to speak for the recently broached ovary, it would demand life, having recently fought for it so fiercely. On Neptune as on earth, women were idealised in inverse proportion to their interests being considered. War was a man's job. Neptunian surgeons clung to the old oath of Hippocrates, which required doctors not to assist women who wanted abortions.

However, there were ways of getting things done on Neptune. Recently the hospitals had had an enquiry from another planet. This planet had a wildly eccentric orbit that not only took it across Neptune's stately orbit round the sun, to lie for long periods inside Neptune, it also swung wildly out of the ecliptic of the other planets in their orderly progression. Neptune welcomed trade with other planets, but Neptunians never went there themselves, relying on the hypnotic pull of Trident City to draw everything they needed from the universe without having to set foot in it. As Neptunians never went up to the surface now, they never bothered themselves about the position of the planets. It was only when the enquiry from Pluto came for live human foetuses, that someone had been sent up to find out where Pluto was. They'd reported back that the planets appeared to be in a fixed line stretching directly from Neptune to the sun, which was eclipsed by them. Pluto was the closest.

This was ideal for such a delicate cargo, and the hospitals had been trying to make contact with Pluto in its wild career for some time. There was initial controversy about the ethics of selling embryos to Plutonians who were an unknown quantity, but the hospitals needed every injection of capital they could get, and Pluto could be a gold-mine.

'We can only offer you an operation where we remove the embryo and transfer it to another support system. We can treat your foetus as a product, which we can market in a normal way. We can't kill it.' Chrissie was confused. She knew what Mudroche the Feely magnate would say: GYMSLIP CRYO MUM IN SHOCK BABY SALE. She didn't know if she could face the hate-mail if she ever went home.

'What, sell my baby?' The surgeon was bored with the ethics of the situation. He said he was sure Pluto was a wonderful place for any baby to grow up.

'You do realise that the financial advantages to you are quite high. You will lose something that is hardly more than a blueprint, that hasn't developed a forebrain, and you will get around fifty *Aitch*.'

Some people said that Plutonians had graveyard breath and were ten foot tall with tinted visors and long dry snake-like tongues, which could reach into a room if they were standing outside. Some said that they were simple homely-looking people like gnomes who would work for years on giant projects which would then come to explosive fruition. The hospital had already agreed with them on the sale, and there was one thing that everybody was agreed on, which was that you didn't mess around with Pluto, not when it was so close.

'It'll go to a good home,' said the surgeon. Chrissie asked if she could see Pluto. The surgeon groaned inwardly. The only piece of sky that Neptunians ever got to see was the bit through the hole above Millionaire's Park, which the space-tour rockets came through. The upward rush of billions of therms of hot, dirty air meant that even the planets were mobile smudges of light, apparently pushed around endlessly like specks of dust in Brownian motion.

'It'll be overhead at midnight, but eclipsed.' Neptunians had long ago abandoned the solar day. 'You won't be able to see anything.' The surgeon made an informed guess at exchange rates. 'In your money, it's worth about ten million pounds.'

It was Betty who reacted at first, keening and holding her hands to her mouth and carrying on as if she'd won freedom from housework for life rather than Chrissie.

'Hey! That lets you off the hook for ever, Chrissie, you realise? With that sort of money you're never going to have to work!' Chrissie, whose whole generation had escaped into cryogenics because nobody wanted their work, looked puzzled for a moment, then caught on. This time, not working meant that she could have anything she liked. Immediately she thought of Betty.

'Betty, I'll buy a house, a big house, will you come and live with me in my house? And we'll go shopping together and we'll buy *everything*. Will you come shopping with me? I'll give you a *million* pounds to come shopping with me. Hey,' Chrissie turned to the surgeon, 'can we have some money now? What's the most expensive drink?'

'Beer,' said the surgeon.

'Well, I'm going to get pissed on *beer*!'

In the ruins of the party below the surgeon found them two beers. Everyone had gone home after the Mood Maid had been switched off, and shaven-headed patients in pyjamas were going round with buckets picking up the syringes. Some of them had plastic-covered transmitters the size of yo-yos taped to their skulls. These, the surgeon explained, were his pet project, the criminally insane psychopaths. Neptune was a society of sensitives, and people who inflicted pain without knowing what they were doing caused untold suffering and the constant escalation of pain. The only treatment at the moment was a constant monitoring of the brainwave patterns.

One of them looked up at Betty and Chrissie from the bucket he was carrying. Betty flinched. His eyes were completely dead.

Chrissie took ten *Aitch* from the surgeon. She looked radiant, ready to go to the party, recreate the freaks, the Mood Maid and the Ganymedes and the 3D mobile abstracts and the surgical pastiche of Siva, and draw them round her with the doctors and psychopaths staring adoringly up her dress as she highkicked and sang on the table, with a few gigawatts of light coming off her dress as if it was the beginning of the first day of creation:

Hey, you

the men would sing, and Chrissie would be moving to the music already, running her hand down the outside of her thigh with the fingers outstretched. She'd hold the radio mike with the other hand and reply with something between a whoop and a scream,

What, Me?

Then the psychopaths would cast down their bucketfuls of syringes, get in line, their faces alive with interest and meaning:

Yes, you!
Space Queen!

And Chrissie would sing:

That's Me?

And the men would sing:

You with the stars in your dress
Dazzling our eyes
Obscene
Every disguise that hides
Anything of you!
Are you ready?

And Chrissie would sing:

The stars are my father
My mother is my soul

And the men would sing:

Oh oh oh oh
Space Queen you can rock and roll
And with your permission
When you've had a little stroll
We can make you a virgin again!
Scoopy-doo!
A virgin again!

And Chrissie would sing:

I can't believe it
I am so happy
This is really happening to me
Is it a dream or
Is it really
Meant to be?

And then they'd all sing all together and mixed-up:

Space Queen!
Bending the rules
Of time and space
Meet your destiny face to face
The moment is right
Astrologically!
Are you ready?

And Chrissie would sing:

The stars are my father
My mother is my soul

Chrissie twirled round in the almost empty carpark, and let go of her handbag. It was almost empty. It caught the lip of the parapet, spun over the edge, and began a gliding, unhurried descent in the general direction of Millionaire's Park. She could always buy another one, or ten, or a hundred handbags, and stuff them full of money, too, if she felt like it, and throw them all off huge tall buildings. As above, so below.

Chrissie and Betty took the lift down for a thousand floors and then started walking and looking at shops. Chrissie bought some chicken and chips, and a red dress for Betty with shoes to match. The material for the red dress was so slinky that it was almost alive and Betty had difficulty keeping it in its box.

'You should have kept it on in the shop,' Chrissie said, licking her fingers free of chicken grease before holding it up to her friend. A warm, dirty gale was blowing along the crowded precinct from the ventilator at the end of the street. It had been sucked up from deep in the interior, and smelt of smuts and cabbages.

'How much did it cost, Chrissie?'

'Not as much as the take-away. Anyway, I *said* I'd give you a million pounds.' Chrissie was looking round for a rubbish bin to dump her Good 'n' Greasy® box in. The chicken had cost $H3.8$, which Chrissie suspected was a lot of money, but Punting had warned them about the price of food.

The pavement on which they were standing began to glow red, then alarmingly it began to undulate. They were standing outside a Mouthy, and had tripped the automatic welcome that rippled the customers persuasively to the darkened interior where the Mouthy machines stood, row upon row of huge inflated lips at waist height. On the right-hand side of the lips was a fruit-machine handle. Some of the lips were closed, and some were open. They were about to get off in haste when the undulation suddenly stopped.

'Ladies! Be my guests! Please stay there as long as you wish with no commitment of any kind!' Chrissie looked down to see the Mouthy proprietor, a legless man sat on a small, exquisite chrome trolley. He had a deeply lined face with intense brown eyes, and he wore a wide check sports coat with padded shoulders. He carried a huge money satchel stuffed with change, like a bookie. He gazed up at Chrissie with a voracious smile of welcome. He had gold teeth, and a diamond was set daintily through his left nostril. He removed his porkpie hat with a flourish from hideously long arms.

'Your presence can only bring me good fortune.' His voice had a gravelly power. He reached up to take Chrissie's empty carton. She instinctively snatched it out of his reach.

'Piss off.' The man immediately lowered his arms to the ground and looked hurt.

'You misunderstand. Please forgive. But, perhaps unawares, you are standing on the forecourt, the *tongue* of my Mouthy. This is not, alas, the most settled of neighbourhoods. I am obliged and honoured to offer you my feeble protection as long as you are on my territory.' Then he started fishing for Chrissie's carton, but she held on to it. 'Tell me, dear lady, how long is it since you have finished your meal? And what did it cost you?' Chrissie had forgotten. She said, counting her change, that the meal and the dress together had come to five *Aitch*.

'Chrissie! That's a million pounds!' Betty was worried that Chrissie had lost her head completely.

'And what will you do with the used container?' asked the Mouthy owner, eyeing the soiled box. When Chrissie had bought it, it had crude moving pictures of chicken frying on the side, with accompanying sizzling noises, but it was almost silent now and the colours were already starting to fade.

'Are you frightened I'm going to chuck litter on your *tongue*?'

'On the contrary, my dear. Would you consider a *sale* of the empty container to me?' There was a heap of empty, rotting boxes in the gutter not ten feet away.

'What about them?' Chrissie pointed.

'Alas, you misunderstand. I wish merely to buy the space where a beautiful young lady once ate her chips from.'

'But I've eaten them,' said Chrissie.

'You misunderstand. I am an artist, and I am looking for artistic experience. Your jealous husband will possess you in what you are, but I can possess you in what you are *not*.' A true Neptunian, the Mouthy owner could now believe he was already holding the box, which did *not* hold the chips, which were already making their way down the divine-looking earthling's longer colon, being excitingly digested; and yes! She would *not* strip off her pretty satin panties to deposit the fibrous waste matter from Uranian potatoes and Venusian chicken, perhaps suspended by leather straps above a glass table, under which he would *not* wriggle and lie at the *Imum Coeli* of the excremental spectacular ... There was no doubt that he was by Neptunian standards, since none of this had happened, an artist of *nothing*. He held up a five *Aitch* note to Chrissie, who took it.

Smiling at the man's gullibility, she handed over the box. Immediately the man attacked the box and tore it in little pieces. At the end, he sighed and rolled his eyes, as if a great release from the commonplace had temporarily come upon him.

'What on earth did you do that for? I've got almost as much money as when I started, and you've got nothing.'

'Young lady, do you not know the value of *nothing*?' the Mouthy owner cried in a terrible voice. He could, perhaps, later amuse himself if there was reluctance on her part by giving her an enema to start the game off. Her friend too, for he had more than one glass table. Afterwards he would give them exquisitely cooked lobster which they would eat naked with chains round their neck by candlelight and then he would pull a lever, the floor would open, and they would fall helplessly into a dark slimy pit full of radioactive crocodiles. Why did they delay? He tugged at Betty's dress, and a bead came off in his hand. He flicked it to the ground.

'Come, come to my house, please. It is so close. I will give you more money.'

'What for?' The man smiled.

'Oh, nothing.' Betty remembered Punting's warning about private houses.

'We don't have enough time, Chrissie.'

'I will buy your time. Allow me please. It will give me so much pleasure. Time is after all, when it is past, another *nothing*.'

'Could I use your toilet to change in, please?' Betty wanted to try on her new dress but the man's mood changed from sunny magnanimity at once.

'No! The reason for my great wealth is that I no longer allow women in my Mouthys. There was a woman once, who broke the code. She wouldn't stay away. We had to cut her arms off, to prevent her burning out any more machines. They are only designed to take the brief spasms of men. But as I said before; accept, please, the protection of my *tongue*. No one will dare harm you.'

The Mouthy owner watched them for a minute, cleaning his nails with a flick knife. Then he went inside. Betty started to change in the subdued glare of the *tongue*, feeling his stare from the darkness burning a hole in her back. She smoothed down her new dress, feeling its rich natural texture and the superb hand-finished seams. Clothes on Earth had been welded, for years. When she looked up she was face to face with Not-Easey.

He had taken his silver bandage off and all there was to show for the brain exchange was a thin pink line across the forehead disappearing into the hairline both sides.

'To break his system I need money. Please be quick. He doesn't recognise me now.' Not-Easey had left the girls to go to work the Mouthys but he hadn't been able to start. Chrissie remembered what he'd said the legless owner had done to his arms in his old body, and immediately gave him the five *Aitch*. It was a million pounds but what the hell.

'Enjoy yourself.' Betty loved her dress. The money Chrissie had given Not-Easey would have paid Betty's rent for as long as the Third Reich had been planned to last, but Betty didn't grudge him a penny of it, as long as Chrissie was enjoying herself. It was only money, after all. And what was that, beside a human life?

Not-Easey changed the note with the Mouthy owner for a coin. The owner kept looking in their direction, and scarcely noticed Not-Easey, who went straight to the highest rolling machine. He wasn't 'that deadly woman'. He looked like just another space cadet, as he slowly put in the coin, bending his gawky body as if he didn't know how to stand against the machine.

Nothing happened when he pulled the lever the first few times. Betty put on her new shoes with high heels, which made the *tongue* wince. A street sweeper went by and gathered up the box which the high heeled shoes had been in and scrunched it noisily into the back pouch. Piled in its bin were the charred mechanical remains of something familiar, as if two humans had melted together in an embrace. It was the rogue Ganymedes, on their way to the infill pits on Millionaire's Park.

The owner seemed to have some control over the *tongue* for it rolled him again to their feet where he stopped, frowning at the dent Betty's heels were making in the surface. Betty foresaw a scene, and asked him quickly, because they were new round there, what *nothing* really consisted of.

'If I may say so, an exquisitely profound question from such a pretty head as your own.' Betty was about to dimple obligingly, if only to buy time so that they could see what happened to Not-Easey's quest, when his machine began to change pitch. And then a nimbus ran round the outline of Easey's body, as if he was silhouetted in neon tubing. He began to writhe, holding on to the padded winner's handles on either side of the Mouthy machine itself.

'*Nothing* is . . . what you have left when you have taken *everything* away. *Nothing* is an active state of bliss, untouched by earthly desire or rancour. The millionaires have access to it, the poor have a dismal parody of it. Do I make myself unclear? How painful . . . *All* transactions are a rehearsal for *nothing*.' Particularly if the girls went to his house, or even if he managed to lure them into the nearby hotel with its trick staircases, floors of razor blades and a snuff cameraman behind every two-way mirror in the suite. There would be a paring down indeed, to *nothing*.

Chrissie couldn't work out why the Mouthy owner hadn't noticed what was going on behind him, but he appeared lost in thought. Not-Easey was surrounded with light, which seemed to be blasting out of the machine. As he stood, which he had for a full half minute, smoke began to roll out of not only his but all the machines, and down across the *tongue*. The Mouthy owner began to be obscured by choking fumes, but he was still intent on philosophy.

'Take myself. *I* have achieved *nothing*. I have become pure. I no longer require anything. I have cleared the space within me.' Not-Easey's clothes appeared to be catching fire. The hessian-covered winner's handles, or 'bugger's grips' as they were called, regardless what was in the mind of the winner, started to steam.

'And now when I have cleared the space within I am free to become a part of nature. That is, not happy, not angry, not wanting. It is like being upon a high place, and being able to look down and see the whole of nature spread out below me, with little fluffy clouds. Yes! I *am* that divine captain –'

The Mouthy owner turned. The noise from Not-Easey's Mouthy was earsplitting; it and all the other Mouthies were going off like a box of fireworks, flaming and drooling bubbles of plastic and electronic circuitry.

'Meet the Maker!' the street people cried, gathering round the *tongue* on a brief, telepathic high, as Not-Easey bucked and swayed. They started to applaud him in a staccato, syncopated rhythm, cheering him on to win against himself in a one-man Saturnalia. The owner's assistant came out choking into the street. He'd been welding plastic cable behind and with a welder's mask and red drops on his apron he looked as if he'd been surprised in the middle of making something *really* nasty.

'It's her again, Harkon, *get the axe*!' screamed the Mouthy owner to the man in the butcher's smock. Harkon turned and lumbered off while the owner jumped up and down in his cart, holding on to the wheels. There was a smashing noise of breaking glass and Harkon reappeared with a fireman's axe. Chrissie didn't see anything you needed to break down with a fireman's axe, but Harkon raised it above his head and turned to Not-Easey. Chrissie screamed as loud as she used to during the fights at closing time outside The Plough on the Wandsworth Road. But Not-Easey was beyond warning, beyond self, lapped in wave upon wave of sensation so that nothing could divert him from his winning streak.

The welder paused uncertainly for a moment and flicked a piece of stray plastic from his moustache. He stepped up to Not-Easey, and spread his legs as if he was going to hit him with the axe. Instead he tapped him on the shoulder. Not-Easey turned round slowly, and then back again. The lights were starting to dim. The welder had his excuse. Measuring the distance carefully, he severed Not-Easey's left arm from the shoulder with one blow. Not-Easey was still standing. The welder moved round Not-Easey to the other side. His mask fell down and he pushed it up again, but he'd lost his sure touch. It took four blows to get the other arm off and when he'd finished Not-Easey was on the floor.

The crowd started to thin and the welder kicked the limbs to the side of the *tongue*. Betty led Chrissie down to the end of the street. Betty felt ill, but Chrissie was actually weeping with shock and horror, saying over and over again, I want to help. Not-Easey had managed to get up somehow and passed them, walking with a curiously lightfooted step towards Millionaire's Park. He glanced at them as he went by and moved away swiftly down the street, as if he didn't need to talk to them, as if the last thing he needed after his arms were chopped off was help.

Betty hurried Chrissie away as Trident Enforcement arrived in their one-man pneumatic tubes from the nearest transit point. The Mouthy owner was still on the spot, and was a prime suspect, still pumping out homicidal vibes. Four of them were giving him a hard time. They stood in a semicircle round him with leathers and crash hats on looking like motorcycle cops in the old tv films. But the hats were to protect extraordinarily enlarged brains which stretched the skull till it was paper thin. They had taken over the owner's nervous system telepathically and he was leaping around on his long hands out of his cart, banging his own head on the ground, screaming stop, stop, I didn't do it. The welding butcher was nowhere to be seen.

On their way back to the hospital the girls passed a deserted tv arcade, where there was a huge panel of tv monitors for every planet in the solar system. A nice-looking young mechanic was eating a sandwich in the middle of the arcade. Betty asked him why almost all the screens were dark, and he said that reception was very bad at the moment. Just to keep Chrissie's mind occupied Betty asked could they see anything from Earth? The mechanic stuffed his sandwich in his mouth and turned knobs for them but all to no avail, until suddenly a figure appeared on the scene in robes. Look, Chrissie, said Betty, feigning interest, it's the *news*! Betty turned the sound up, and it was the Burning Judge.

'You, Carwash, are a bitter lesson to the state. You were placed in a position of trust and responsibility –' The reception faded again. The earth in both universes was exactly the same, still.

Juanita the surgeon's wife slipped into her sterile, one-piece C-throo operating gown, dipped her gold pendant chain in surgical spirit and hung the tiny cross around her slim neck before it had a chance to dry off. Then she buttoned the collar tight. She always changed in the surgeon's office with its view of the head of the river flowing through Millionaire's Park. The Park was also a municipal dump which rose constantly and unevenly. Finally the weight of rubbish would set off a minor collapse of levels somewhere in the interior and a whole subcity would be squashed. The Park would judder down a couple of hundred feet, a few surrounding buildings would fall and the process would start again. The waste from the city had been threatening to fill the great bowl for years, but time after time Neptune was shaken with tremors and the Park subsided to something like its old level. The buildings on either side had to keep building upwards to keep pace with this and their foundations moved further and further down with each sinking of the plateau. Some streets had acquired a headroom of four or five feet but were still busy with pimps and muggers, frantically trying to get a break before the city buried them for ever. The compacted debris had deep internal fires, and there were stories of salamanders.

Juanita tucked the ends of the transparent trousers into the tops of the clear plastic galoshes and tossed her pretty head at herself in the mirror. She had been a student arsonist whom the surgeon had saved. Criminals were not solar impacted as the sun had no real place in the imaginations of Neptunians, they were merely matter-reduced and allowed to revert to this dimension inside out. Public criminals like arsonists were then set loose in Millionaire's Park. The surgeon had saved one and completely rebuilt her, turning a rather mousy-looking political activist into an exact copy of his most lubricious fantasy; tautbellied, pertnosed, with breasts a miracle of engineering, and a black silky bush which now showed a dark smudge through the trousers, a tiny thicket which the surgeon could never decide looked better on or off.

When he'd finished, Juanita had given up her politics and married him, but there were still strange kinks in her thinking. They were small matters and it would be the grossest Neptunian insult if he were ever to lay his wife out on the table and remove a set of memories from her mind. But she had claimed to have 'lived' in cryo, and passed in that life into a universe where *out of all the planets, only the earth was inhabited*, and the people there had the dimmest folk-memory of the racial attributes of the other planets.

Her brother had been a mathematician of great brilliance, who had proved that matter-reduction required an alternate universe to absorb the excess matter, which flowed into the universe under conditions of excess cold such as preceded reduction, in the same way that at the same subzero temperatures, liquid gas could not be held in a glass test-tube, but would flow through the walls of its previously impermeable container. If you got near enough to the ultimate zero, you could always break on through to the other side. However he had lost his reason, and stood in for someone at a bankruptcy burial in Millionaire's Park, and was now half a mile down with the salamanders. So he was unable to prove his sister sane, and she had learnt to keep quiet about 'other' worlds.

The surgeon was wearing white kneeboots and jodhpurs, with a white peaked cap. The operating theatre which he showed to Betty and Chrissie was all his: lasers and lights set in a big dish over the table so that the video could catch every moment for playing back to the students. It was a small room though with a low ceiling, and Juanita was the only assistant, and she sat down with Chrissie to prepare her for the operation. They were selling to a first-time buyer so everything had to be just right. The surgeon liked giving her things like this to do – it gave her life a sense of purpose, and he could keep an eye on her.

'Now, Christine,' Juanita was saying in her soft, clear voice. 'You haven't been exposed to any radioactive sources, have you?'

Every day, on earth, enough plutonium was stolen or lost to poison the whole of the human race, and much of it was doing just that. Chrissie put from her mind the poisoned water tables, the scorchingly radioactive seas, and shook her head dully.

'No.' Juanita's little silver micropencil, with the light on top that blinked if you lied, signalled that Chrissie was telling the truth. Chrissie wanted it to be the truth, because she wanted to live, or at least not go back into cryo. Juanita, gifted like many who came back from cryo with a sight of the past and the future, saw that Chrissie was in fact from her earth, the one that stood alone in space. She saw Chrissie coming through cryo the other way, and knew the answer to the next question before she asked it.

'Have you at any time been cryogenically frozen?'

There was a long pause. Chrissie swallowed. They both knew she was going to lie.

'No she hasn't,' said Betty. The surgeon, busy setting up, said let Chrissie answer for herself please.

'I was, once. For about ten minutes.'

'And were you matter-reduced during this time?' Juanita kept her thumb over the little light so that everything would go all right for Chrissie. But she said yes, she had been matter-reduced, it was when she was fifteen.

'It's after she's pregnant. You've got to find out if she was matter-reduced after she was pregnant. That's the point of the questionnaire.' Juanita's fixed smile never wavered.

'And were you pregnant when you were matter-reduced?' She put her finger over the little light again.

'No,' said Chrissie. The little light glowed pinkly through Juanita's slender, translucent fingers. The surgeon watched it and exchanged looks with Juanita. Chrissie asked nervously if anything was the matter. Juanita explained to her, as if she didn't know, that anyone who came back from matter-reduction had an even chance of having their chromosome chains exchanged for a three-dimensional mirror-image, even if there was no exchange of characteristics with the foetus. So the foetus could be sterile.

'Is there something the matter?' Betty asked.

'Christine, I'm afraid you haven't been telling the truth. The embryo's been through matter-reduction, hasn't it?' Chrissie began to cry. The surgeon stopped his preparations suddenly and started turning off the lights. He was angry at Juanita's deception. He knew more about the penalties exacted by nature as the price animals paid for matter-reduction. He'd had to rebuild Juanita from scratch over fifteen years. Like most reducees, she had come back left-handed, with her frontal brain lobes having changed functions. Perhaps this accounted for her misplaced sense of kinship with the patient, as she attempted to cover up the lie. The surgeon was shocked by the double dishonesty. He'd rather suffer the Plutonian lawyers to raze the hospital for not fulfilling contract then let the women get away with conspiracy.

'Could you see them at the desk and pay back the advance?' The surgeon opened the door and the echoes of the lobby could be heard. The operating theatre was three airlocks down in the hospital and had looked out on Millionaire's Park a hundred and fifty years ago. It was big and spacious with pink marble floors and a vaulted ceiling, and doors at the end which were shuttered with steel to stop them bursting open with the weight of all the rubbish and earth piled miles high above them. He motioned Chrissie outside. Chrissie knew that crying was no good and she stopped and stared him in the eye.

'I've spent it.'

The three women looked at the surgeon, willing him to call off his bluff. Both Juanita and Chrissie *knew* this wasn't how the story ended. The surgeon knew too, in his heart.

'We can't do it. It's selling potentially shoddy goods to a first-time buyer.' Pluto had previously been of such little interest that Neptunians were slow to wake up to the fact that not only was it the nearest planet, but that it was engaged together with all the other planets in some weird stasis, and that, further, the Neptunians who bought old reflecting telescopes in pawnshops and made the long, unfamiliar trek up to the surface discovered that the zodiac itself appeared to have been hastily swivelled round. The Neptunians were now the last thing between the solar system, stretched out like a line of uneven marker buoys, and the constellation of Aries. The unease had begun as a storm of protest over poor reception of a popular Martian tv series. It had been a snuff-opera, and Mars had been eclipsed by Saturn, Jupiter, Uranus and Pluto just as the knives were drawn. After some hours, it became apparent that *nothing* in the solar system appeared to be moving, and this had been coincident (the surgeon calculated) with the arrival of this troublesome girl. Was this forcefield blackmail by Pluto? Had they got him on peeper? The surgeon couldn't see any suspiciously large motes of dust floating in the room, the traditional method of Neptunian espionage.

Again, perhaps it was the earthlings who were organising it. The surgeon, whose oversubtle mind had a nose stronger than any paranoiac's for sniffing out conspiracy, felt trapped, but was unable to feel where the conspiracy was coming from. If only he could have rearranged his wife's temporal lobes and combed out every ingrown synapse, then she wouldn't have turned against him. 'Bloody hell,' said Betty quietly, 'all she wants is an abortion, can't you see that?'

The surgeon had already been told of the early arrival of Pluto's freighter. It had docked without permission on the space port at the edge of Millionaire's Park, a big, black sturdy spacecraft. The sigyl of the planet, the horned cross bearing the ball between the cusps, was flaking off the nose. No one had seen it come, and it had only been discovered at the spaceport after several loud bangs had been recorded in the vicinity. There were no lights in the craft. The Neptunians had politely placed a gangway capable of bearing several tons per square inch outside what might equally well have been the airlock or the main drive-motor exhaust. Nothing had happened. But having offered them a little foetal plaything, it was difficult for the surgeon now to cry scruples and leave them with nothing. If Juanita hadn't deceived him, he could have overlooked it. For this, he'd take her little bush away for sure.

Suddenly the surgeon realised that he was looking the conspiracy straight in the face. It was being created entirely by the women for their own ends. Secretly he breathed a sigh of relief. After all, there were always ways of dealing with women. He opened his mouth but Betty spoke first.

'I'll have a word with you, alone.' And then Chrissie and Juanita had melted away together into the echoing hall as if on castors and had closed the door, twice, the first time having caught one of the strings of Chrissie's operating gown.

Betty lay down on the operating table and hitched up her dress. The surgeon didn't move. She reached out and turned the operating lights down low. She took her shoes off and started to pull her knickers off. The surgeon looked at her face and it was filled with hatred. Betty started to unbutton her suspenders. With

127

each unclipping the surgeon's unease increased. I don't want, said Betty acidly, to take up too much of your precious time. You could pay back the advance with malachite, said the surgeon, if you've got any, it's worth more than gold here.

Betty took her dress off over her shoulders, dropping it on top of the matching red high-heeled shoes whose pressure points twinkled when you walked.

'No, I haven't got any malachite.' The surgeon had been faithful to the image he'd made of Juanita, and noted critically the deviations from the divine norm of his wife's shapely body. Who did Betty think she was, offering him her dry beaver in complete contempt?

'This is to pay you,' she said. 'For Chrissie to have the abortion. Understand?'

The surgeon took out a silver box from a cupboard in the half dark and put it down by the table. He plugged it in and started to draw thick, flattish wires out of one end, covered in studs, and suction pads. *What have I let myself in for?* thought Betty.

The surgeon had matched her clinical approach with his own and now she was scared. Praying that the other two hadn't gone away, Betty said, I don't want to take up too much of your precious time, but what do you want? The surgeon smiled, and asked if she was *afraid*. This was a Feely camera, but it didn't just take stills like on earth, it was a continuous monitor of all her bodily reactions. He draped the studs and suckers over her, twining them round her legs and shoulders and round her breasts. Betty lay back glumly as if it was the dentist's and waited for the drilling to begin. It was a Feely movie then, so he could replay her heaving loins when she was gone. Betty said bravely that no, she wasn't afraid. The surgeon said that it was important that she was a *little* bit afraid.

The Feelies were to do with his pet programme, the surgeon explained. The men in pyjamas who you saw clearing up the party, they have no will of their own, they are *Xontrolled*. The problem with the men, and it was nearly always men, was that they did not know what they were doing. They were psychopaths, and that, on a planet as intuitive and dreamily sensitive as Neptune, created an extraordinary problem.

'If you know what you're doing, then you will suffer the consequences of your action. But if there are social elements who are unable to relate to the ethics of their anti-social behaviour, then you will get *pain inflation*. The psychic economics of Neptune are self contained. We can't take more pain than we can digest, we can't like you do on earth for instance, radiate it away into space. What we do, is to make a Feely, and then we put the psychopaths *in your body and mind*.' The surgeon taped two electrodes to Betty's temples. 'I mean the Feely that you leave behind. These will read what you're thinking. You do consider yourself sensitive, don't you?'

Betty was annoyed at the surgeon's speedy, self-involved preciousness. She started to feel contempt for him. There was always some ulterior motive, some dubious social theology for these creeps to dress up their masturbatory fantasies.

'So what's the deal? Will you do the other operation if I let you read my mind?' The surgeon nodded and began unbuttoning his coat.

Betty worked out that it was her safe period and unless he got even weirder all she had to fear was some routine before he got it on with her. He was turned away in the corner of the room, lighting a cigarette. He came over and offered it to her. Betty took it. She was nervous, and when she was nervous she always wanted something in her lungs whether it was a joint or a cigarette. One of the girls at the flat smoked the government's own reefers, Brown Windsor, but Betty preferred tobacco.

She sucked in gratefully but then realised that the cigarette had something else in it. The room immediately began to ripple and writhe, and the snakes on her body appeared to be climbing up towards her. Any moment she expected to pass out. The shitty surgeon had given her one full of STP, which was harder and faster than acid, according to its adherents in the prisons, and under Waterloo Bridge. The surgeon bulged and swayed and his eyebrows started to drift around his face. Betty tried to keep her vision by blinking rapidly but this only made them worse. The surgeon smiled idiotically at her.

'This won't take a moment,' he said. She had completely lost any sense of time, and had forgotten her companions at the door. The surgeon went back to the corner. Betty imagined him in the corner like a mole, digging something nasty out of the earth. Why had he turned his back on her for so long? Had she done something wrong?

'What am I doing here? I don't understand what I'm doing here.' Betty wanted to move to get up but the Feely suckers seemed to be suddenly tense, and the Feely was humming, probably ready to devour her if she moved, and spit the mangled image out the other side. Betty felt powerless. Then because she was about to be humiliated she felt guilty. *Nice girls don't get into situations like this.*

The surgeon put some hideous music on, like a novice orchestra of people playing saws. Betty's stomach turned to jelly. *If I shit myself maybe he won't come near me.* But then, Chrissie wouldn't get what she was here for either.

'Please, I don't feel well, I want to go to the bathroom.' He didn't move away from his dark corner. Betty thought she should have kept her mouth shut rather than own up, or threaten the monster in the room with having any orifices at all. But he hadn't heard. He was chuckling. He stood up slowly in the corner of the room and turned round. Betty saw that it wasn't the surgeon at all, he had gone down the hole at the corner of the room, it was in fact a giant ape in a surgeon's coat with huge hairy hands, making its way towards her. She tried to sit up again but the Feely stickers were hard as iron and held her down. Betty screamed.

Then suddenly Chrissie and Juanita were in the room, and the lights were on and the surgeon was taking off the mask while Juanita helped dress her, and the surgeon was saying, it's all right, you did very well, he was so *sorry* that the people who made the programme for the hospital couldn't be told anything in advance, or they would not be as afraid. Juanita whispered that he could not use Neptunians because everyone knew about the programme, and that she had had it done to her once, but that the surgeon was a *good man*. She was shaking and sat by Chrissie's side to hold her hand as much out of self-support as support for Chrissie.

Chrissie's eyes were half closed. She'd had something to loosen her up and she said it was lovely, gorgeous, and told Betty not to look so worried for her, Chrissie was going to be all right. Betty's hallucinogenics were subsiding quickly and she mostly felt angry at being cheated and used. The surgeon patted her on the shoulder although he was busy, and said it was a good take, and that she'd paid in full now: he knew it wasn't any picnic.

The surgeon thought the girl from earth was looking uncommonly sulky, as if she didn't like helping. He was always putting his reputation on the line for people, cutting corners, trying to include philanthropy. All that happened in the end was that you upset the weaker brethren who didn't want you to plan their lives or interfere but he wasn't going to let that upset him. She was pretty lucky that they hadn't had time to go the whole hog, but the time was too tight. Still he'd added another tape to his pet project and the exchange looked as if the host mother, as Chrissie appeared on the consent form, was a healthy specimen.

'We're all fair and square now. Time is money you say; we say, time is pain. It is pain that drives the moons of Mars backwards against the solar clock. Time is pain, for time is fear, time is terror. Pleasure is timeless. If my project with the mentally ill succeeds, it is possible we will abolish pain, which in its turn will abolish Time itself...'

Betty held on to Chrissie's hand as she lay on the operating table and Juanita gave her another 'tiny' injection, 'to make her forget'. She offered the sweet little syringe to Betty as well, who looked at its dripping end askance and said thanks, she'd rather remember. It was only a memory drug, Juanita said: by the time that we get it, pain is already a memory from the body, which the drug simply blocked. Betty was still reeling from the first hallucinogenic and needed all the memory she could muster of what it was like normally. So like someone sitting on a sharp stone to keep themself awake, Betty was allowed to stay with Chrissie.

'If you cut me, can you do it below the bikini line?'

The surgeon was putting on elbow-length polythene gloves, and he paused, looking puzzled. Without any interest in sun, or sea, or Pacific atolls to name clothes after, the last thing he was thinking of doing was making Chrissie look good for the beach. Chrissie pointed to her stomach.

'Mine's about here.' Chrissie couldn't understand how he was so *thick*. 'You do it when you're sunbathing.' She turned to Juanita. 'Tell him about sunbathing. Is he stupid?'

Juanita suddenly remembered the earthly seas in all their blue majesty, the line where the infinite waters met the infinite air, and she felt a wrenching sadness. All they had in Neptune was Inner Space. Don't get angry, Juanita whispered to Chrissie, relax. Anger is time, the surgeon intoned, anger is pain. Juanita pressed Chrissie back on the table, looked at her iris, and told her to count.

'Count what?' Juanita said, count anything, count the numbers themselves if you like, beginning at one. When the drug worked the patient stayed in the present and so was unable to think beyond the number one.

The surgeon was putting Chrissie's legs in inspection stirrups. Betty nervously asked him if possible not to shave Chrissie, that she'd asked not to be shaved. Neptunian hospitals had for years counted hair, and pubic hair especially, as a true friend of hygiene, after tests showing how it carried the body's electrolytic field; in fact the breakthrough had been made so long ago it was no longer part of medical history that it had been otherwise, ever. The surgeon replied patiently, careful not to irritate the Earthlings with their bizarre requests, that he was not going to shave Chrissie anyhow, because she didn't have a beard. Betty rolled her eyes, and the surgeon muttered to Juanita that these two sounded completely crazy. Later, reading in the *Encylopaedia Solaris*, he read that the Bikini Atoll was where the first nuclear bombs were exploded. Plainly, then, the 'bikini' must be a garment for protecting the vital parts against radioactive irradiation, and in a nuclear society such as earth's would be worn the whole time.

'Who's Pluto?' Chrissie asked.

'Pluto's the government of Pluto. They're paying.'

'What's he like? Pluto?' The surgeon wished he could concentrate on what he was doing and the patient could be mumbling the First Number. To Betty's critical eye the box of instruments beside him as he worked looked rather like earthly knives and forks.

'Pluto? Oh, he's a charming chap.' Juanita's lie detector flashed and she turned it off. In the hour which Chrissie and Betty had spent away the supply of information on Pluto had gone away to almost nothing. They were violently destructive. They were violently regenerative. They were individually clever. They only made their effects felt as mass movements. The planet had been completely silent since the dispatch of the freighter, which was itself as quiet as the grave. The hospital had not yet established an exchange point or the currency in which they were to be paid. Pluto ruled atomic fission, and the surgeon had uneasy feelings that the ship might take off simply leaving a few thousand gallons of radioactive slops from whatever they were doing in there. But then again, the Plutonians were said to work with gold, and maybe they had asteroid-belt factories turning the useless stuff out by the dream-mile. If only the hospitals could get Neptune back on the gold standard, they could control inflation, and begin to pay some attention to the hideous social conditions of the Interior. The surgeon's probe moved inside Chrissie's uterus preparing to detach the embryo from the wall. But she wouldn't lie still.

'Chrissie, count to one.'

'But I thought that Pluto ran the underworld. That's what someone said.' Neptune had been buzzing with rumours ever since the arrival of the black freighter. Betty looked to see what the surgeon was doing, with his hideous knives and forks and spoons. What she saw almost made her faint. Instead of going into the uterus from the vagina, the surgeon was standing between Chrissie's legs, and without having made any incision at all, was passing his hands in and out of her body above the pelvic girdle. As soon as he withdrew his hand, the flesh closed up. He kept looking down as if he could see through the flesh to what he was doing, like a man patiently threading a needle with both hands underwater. Betty tried blinking again but he was still there. The Neptunians had found some way to give the powers that were called psychic surgery on earth to anyone, and took it completely for granted. Chrissie sat up again. The surgeon looked up irritated.

'What's the underworld?'

'It's a nightclub,' Juanita said, trying to get her to lie down. If Chrissie leapt around much more he'd make a mistake. It was already difficult enough because the prize was so tiny.

'Is Pluto the father? If he's not the father, why's he taking it?'

'Count to one, there's a good girl,' said the surgeon. Juanita injected her with another half-cc. of Anti-Mnemosyne, right in the jugular, and had the needle out again before Chrissie knew she'd been injected. At the same time, the lights in the operating theatre started to get darker somehow. There seemed to be a glow coming from underneath Chrissie's pelvic girdle, or maybe with the surgeon's hands right through her it was coming through the flesh as well, but the rest of the lights were starting to dim to red. As the drug worked on Chrissie, so it dismantled her sense of identity, dissolving the walls of the self, so that like the broken Cryos, she flowed down to mingle with all the souls that ever were, and listen to the doleful music of the first Noble Truth, that all is sorrow: and then she thought, *I want my baby*. Betty and Juanita held a hand each, as Chrissie drowned in the collective sorrow of humanity. Chrissie cried. Pluto ruled Hades, and the grim god had summoned a part of her it seemed to squeak and gibber, too soon, on the dimly lit plains of the dead. Chrissie hung on with all her might, and like a dying roadie trying to test a sound system, whispered one, one, one, as the lights went down and down in the room, till there was only the glow from the surgeon's optical probe and then that went too.

It was probably another woman got in a Mouthy, the surgeon thought. The piecemeal administration of Neptune meant that the electricity was always on the verge of giving out and Mouthy jackpots were often the final straw that would plunge whole districts into dark for days. They were quite safe this deep in the hospital but the emergency generators sometimes took hours to crank up. What worried the surgeon more than anything, though, was if their clients had disembarked and got caught in a nocturnal free-fire zone between two or more gangs, who often took the opportunity of the dark to settle a few scores. But then again, perhaps *they* were like bulletproof armadillos who moved around obliviously in their radioactive burrows under blankets of lead a foot thick. Certainly, the footings on the freighter platform had had to be reinforced since the ship arrived; there was certainly something about either the crew or the ship that was *heavy*, in a way that was strictly out of this world.

'Have you got a light? I'm almost there.' Juanita lit a Lucifer, one of the smelly, sulphurous flares that passed for emergency lighting when that part of the hospital was built. The blue flame crackled and snapped like an arc-weld. Suddenly there was a great noise outside, of falling masonry. Then there were massive steps in the stone hall. One, two, three. One, two, three. Juanita struggled to light a second Lucifer off the first as it began to die but the second wouldn't take. The first flare seemed to have sucked all the oxygen from the room, and as it died, the air felt chokingly thick, and heavy.

The surgeon had almost completed a graft on to a support system that would be handed over to the purchasers, when the Lucifer failed and Juanita struggled with matches. He was puzzled by the noise in the hall. It was almost as if the old doorway had collapsed. Certainly, something was now in the hall. He completed the transfer by the last match which burnt Juanita's fingers. She let it fall to the ground with a little cry. He'd obviously made the fingers too sensitive.

The surgeon straightened up with the support system now hermetically sealed round the embryo. The job was finished and he was going to have to give it to whatever was the other side of the door. He opened the door a crack. It was completely dark outside. There was definitely something breathing out there. Whatever it was had a somewhat archaic sense of direction, because it had walked, or swum, through a hundred and fifty years of detritus and then burst through the old door. But the surgeon had nerves of steel, and he held the little manmade cradle out into the reeking darkness, asking them to adhere to the currency rates of exchange for noon that day, forgetting that neither planet could see the sun.

A square illuminated tray appeared under his outstretched arm, and the surgeon put the box on it. There was the noise of coin on marble, and the footsteps again. Then there was a scraping, as something drew itself over the shattered steel doors at the end, back the way it came.

The lights came on. The Lucifers had left a smoky strata of blue in the upper half of the hall, and the old doors at the end had indeed been taken down by something walking in at the old level from the outside. It probably didn't come down the new staircases because they would break under the weight, the surgeon thought.

Betty and Juanita came out with Chrissie on the trolley. The surgeon smiled at Chrissie, who was still going one, one, one. Betty of course wasn't a patient and so he was completely serious when he looked at her and said *that* was all taken care of, and Juanita would be at their disposal for another fifteen minutes, and would provide Chrissie with instructions in the unheard-of event of any internal bleeding. The girls went in the lift together and the surgeon ran to something in the corner which had just caught his eye. It was a pile of gold coins. They were big, yellow, heavy in the hand, with an armadillo-like creature on one side, while on the other the cross of matter sat below the half circle of desire, and the full circle of its resolution: the glyph of Pluto.

Betty and Chrissie found themselves in Millionaire's Park. The hospital shuttle ran to the Park and back again, carrying the raped, and mutilated and the *nothing*-volunteers anywhere they wanted to go, provided it was either the hospital or the Park. Betty and Chrissie got off at the end of the line too late to see the Plutonian freighter make the rubbish shimmer with a triple sonic boom that shook the infill down six inches, adding, so the prophets of ¡*doom!* declared, only another week to the period of grace when the Park would touch the ceiling of the great dome. In Neptunian eyes the prospect of living on the surface was viewed with horror. It was like going back to the Stone Age. Tridenters who lived round the Park would rather be banished to the Interior, with its slave labour and earthquakes.

The smell of the exhaust loitered in the hollows where Betty took Chrissie for warmth. It had suddenly got cold with the freighter leaving. They had no coats. Betty had a little map which said if they walked for what looked like ten miles over to the other side they could get to the surface and back to ZV-3, but Chrissie huddled in the acrid pong of the hollow and wouldn't move another step. In despair for her friend, Betty went to the lip of the hollow and stared down into the river as it cut its way through layer upon layer of rising garbage, like a tiny version of the Grand Canyon. Grass never had time to grow before the bulldozers swept out yet another layer of rubbish over the surface. The Park was illuminated from arclights round the giant central hole, but the Plutonian exhausts hung heavily in the air, making a thin, mean fog. Betty jumped. A figure appeared beside her, waving long arms by its side. But the head looked familiar. It was Not-Easey. He had got another pair of arms somewhere, and they hung loosely at his side.

Chrissie saw Not-Easey and came out of the hollow and looked around.

'Why's it like it is?' she asked him. Not-Easey shrugged; hardly a convincing gesture in his state.

'This is how Millionaire's Park has always been,' he began slowly. 'Millionaires were never bankrupted on Neptune. Instead, when they no longer could command credit, they were buried alive under the infill of their possessions. Houses, helicopters, and their servants the working poor, were all bulldozed over their owners. It was moral, for they had failed. It was also deflationary. It wiped out millions of *Aitch* at a stroke, took it permanently out of circulation, turned all that wealth to *nothing*.'

Rivulets of dry dust moved slowly down the lip of the river's valley, laboriously trickling through or past beds, old tvs and household robots. Chrissie thought she saw another bead dress like hers, but when she looked closely it was falling apart at the seams, and Not-Easey with his long, unwieldy arms hauled her back from the edge before the section broke off and slid in a mess of wire and polythene sacking to form a little dam across the bottom.

Not-Easey pointed to a row of holes near the river. Apparently after years of turning inverts loose in the Park, they had with their reversed-out genetic coding managed to hang on and start a colony down by the river. They were frequently troubled by gangs and the edge of the river was sometimes boobytrapped to discourage the inquisitive.

Easey rubbed his hands together. They were white, since no one had black hands on Neptune. In the distance, a little rollicking figure detached itself from the huge buildings and started to climb over the uneven terrain towards them. Soon they could hear singing which left no doubt as to who it was. It was Punting, utterly unsurprised to see them gathered there, singing a sea-shanty.

'*For the raging seas did roar,*
And the stormy winds did blow
And we jolly sailor-boys were sitting up aloft,

And the land-lubbers lying down below, below, below
And the land-lubbers lying down below!

'Ahoy there, me hearties,' he said. Then he looked round at the waste all around and shook his head. 'What a bloody mess,' he said. His shirt front was stained red.

Punting had gone straight to an old stamping ground, the *O-E-¼*, and booked himself into a little club where he was able to drink a lot of gin and later on buy a first-rate ticket in the front row of a local videobuggery competition. The object of videobuggery was to send a radio-controlled probe as far as possible up your opponent's anus. The probe had a little tv lens which filmed the progress up the colon and the monitors could guide the contestants and tell them if they were sending their probe in the right direction. It was all much posher than his local club at home and they had two little naked chaps from the lower depths dancing round the ring, bollock-naked, with both their hands on a radio console trying to leap their way out of trouble. When the probe penetrated, you could see the fellows doing double somersaults, trying to foul up the other fellow's inertial guidance system.

Later when they both had probes up them, and were springing up and down, Punting had never laughed so much in his life. Everybody else was dead serious. Then suddenly Punting found out why. There was a loud clap, or a smack, and Punting's shirtfront suddenly changed colour. Peering into the haze, Punting saw one of the little chaps almost apart in the middle, only held together by a few strands of his backbone. And there was all this blood everywhere. It had been *snuff*-videobuggery! Punting was basically quite a decent sort of chap and didn't quite know what to think, especially when a Neptunian worthy climbed into the ring and started to take his pleasure with one end of the late contestant.

The winner, in order to attract attention away from this feat, dropped his radio-controlled probe in a box of explosives which were meant to be used for later contestants. When nobody applauded him, he seized his dead opponent's radio console and detonated the probe. There were going to be thirty other bouts that evening so there was a fair old stash of cordite in the tray. Punting was blown through a wall, down an alley, and through another wall. As usual, he was unharmed, due to his '*abominable good luck*'. He was going to go straight into another club, just to get his nerve back, when suddenly he found himself surrounded by Trident Enforcement, who made him run to Millionaire's Park. He somehow felt that the group by their solemn faces wasn't ready for the full story. They did look glum, certainly. Punting lifted up one of Not-Easey's arms sympathetically. The poor boy had had to have a replacement. You either had to cry, or laugh. Punting laughed.

'Did you go for a Chinese meal, old boy?'

Betty explained that it was – mostly – Easey's body but definitely Not-Easey's brain. She pointed to the thin pink line of the forehead.

'Well, is it coming back with us?' Punting asked, anxious not to lose the outward appearance of an engineer. My body wants to go, Not-Easey said dully, but my mind wants to stay.

'Oh dear, oh dear. We're going to need a proper engineer, not someone slapped together with bits and pieces from the cat's-meat man.' Not-Easey said he was coming anyway, because he'd been identified as an alien, but they shouldn't worry, because everything on their ship had been taken care of and they wouldn't need an engineer. And he pointed to the great hole that led to the sky.

Lit from below, a tiny space-freighter was descending towards them, on a gossamer wire. It was tracked so well by searchlights that they could already read the ship's number on the freshly polished hull. As it came closer it looked less like the return of ZV-3 than the tv flagship for 'Safe Among The Stars', which of course was only a model, or the special one which was only used for solar impact drops when they were shown on tv. *The Fair Viol* winked in the lights as she descended on the winch.

'The others will be here soon too,' said Not-Easey.

Punting's eyes weren't too good over twenty-five yards to be quite honest, and at first he thought the object was another planetary body moving to the wrong position, as they seemed to have done with great regularity on the trip so far. But by digging his old bifocals out and craning up he could see the ship descending, with a halo round her caused by the fog.

'Last night the moon had a silver ring,
And tonight no moon we see!
The skipper he laughed a hearty laugh
And a hearty laugh laughed he!

'It looks like there's a storm brewing,' Punting concluded. He turned and saw Shorter beside him. Shorter was a true meteorologist. Shorter didn't think you'd get much weather, to speak of, because the hot air was always going out of the hole. Shorter looked at Punting, who was an interesting colour, what with the blood and the brick-dust, and shifted a package from under one arm to the other.

'And now the last one is coming,' Not-Easey intoned. 'They have put you all on a gestalt frequency.'

Punting was examining Shorter's purchase. It was a hideous ornamental toasting fork in the shape of a trident, made of wrought iron, with a plastic inlay on the handle which said *A Present From Neptune*. Shorter had been told to hand over his wallet by a gang of muggers, and had unwrapped it to defend his few pence and his honour to the last, whereupon the muggers had fled, believing that their intended victim had suddenly produced the fateful ray-gun whose beam inverted its targets. Shorter used it as a pointer to where the colony of bona fide inverts were glumly unblocking the river which had been dammed accidentally by Chrissie. Their lungs flapped laboriously on their chests and they were sheeted in polythene to stop their intestines tearing on the old bicycle wheels and sub-frame assemblies that poked out of the side of the rubbish.

'What's *that*?' The inverts heard his voice and looked up. Though hideous to look at, skinless and with twisted sinew and bone, they had made a life for themselves which was easier than the turmoil of Neptune. They raised children and had everything they needed every time a millionaire went down. To warm their burrows they had the legendary salamander, a creature that dwells in fire. Their life was long and leisurely, and they only feared to go back. They also thought Shorter was pointing the fateful ray-gun which would have turned them back into the mainstream of Trident City, and they fled to their burrows with guttural barks and piping cries.

True to Not-Easey's prediction, Pagey arrived. The bags under his eyes were even larger than before, and he had a wet apron on which he took off and threw down wearily on the ground.

'All right, what's going on then? What's the game?' Punting turned to Pagey. He refused to be surprised by the so-called superior predictions of Easey. He'd probably just seen Pagey coming.

'It's the gestalt frequency,' Punting said straightfaced. Then he laughed. In fact Punting had taken on board so much Gordon's that he was insulated very well against the gestalt frequency, which was why he'd been bum-bailiffed by the Thought police, in desperation. Punting thought that the second Easey, if indeed there had been a change, was just as much a pompous Mr Knowall as the first, and didn't listen to his explanation of the life-cycle of the inverts.

'All right, so why have they gathered us all together, then?' Sooner or later he'd make a mistake and then by George they'd teach him his place. Easey replied with infuriating patience, condescending and world-weary.

'When you landed, the planets were somehow lined up. But then we noticed that after you landed, they remained lined up. We didn't pay much attention at first. But somehow, your arrival has stalled the clock.' He held out his watch. It was an open pair of lips, with the hands coming out of the mouth. The second hand moved with great sluggishness.

'Time only continues by our will. Because Time is slowing down, before Pain is annihilated, we run the risk, should you stay, of Time's entropy ceasing entirely at a high level of pain.' There was no trace of the wretched aesthete, now. Not-Easey had suddenly become spokesman for a whole planet. Punting asked, did he mean that they were being *thrown out*?

'I'm coming too, though.' He seemed to be in communication with them, somehow, pausing before he spoke. 'But they say they'll come and get me.'

'When?' Punting asked. Not-Easey started to walk over to the steps that led up to the freighter platform, where the ZV-3 was now sitting in front of an absurdly tiny ramp.

'When the time is right.'

The Neptunians had worked the ship over inside and out. They had repaired the cracked steering wheels, fitted a totally new pilot's window, and somehow had got all the Cryos back in bottles with the cooling fans on. Betty laughed to see how clean it was. Even the flying duck transfers had been lovingly restored. Pagey had a full box of ammunition. All the controls were on standby, as if the best crew of engineers in the universe had just finished with her. The tanks read three-quarters full. Punting reached under his seat to find not one but two full bottles of 'Glen Glasgow'. Not-Easey told them to get strapped in for take-off, and they dumbly obeyed him, although there was no way, as Shorter knew, that they could clear Neptune unless they had an induction-ring assisted launch.

Betty checked in the food compartment and there were tins and tins of tiny Neptunian portions of food, someone had gone out and bought at least $H50$'s worth of groceries for them. All the dud bulbs had been replaced, and there was even a cushion with a mermaid on it for Chrissie to lie on as she didn't have a seat. But the plastic lobsters and the mermaid skin had gone. Shorter reckoned that they must know what they were doing, because they'd repaired the broken springs in the co-pilot's seat and any-one who had gone to that amount of trouble, *and* re-covered the places where the foam plastic burst through, wasn't fooling about. They were going to get shot of ZV-3, P.D.Q., and if what Not-Easey was saying was correct, they needed to because normal entropy during their visit had almost entirely ceased. Shorter looked down at his watch. It seemed to be going at the right speed to him, but he was well enough up on relativity to know that that meant very little. Though for what exact little it meant, he'd have to wait a few weeks till the 'R' instalment of the *Reader's Digest Encyclopaedia of Space*. He looked out through the spanking new pilot's video unit at the great buildings of the city, fringeing the park. Chrissie stood behind him and he turned and smiled at her. The kid looked a bit pale, but she actually smiled back. Then they looked out together on the web of laser, plasma and neon that wove Trident City out of the night as the big lights slowly dimmed overhead.

'Did you get what you wanted, Chrissie?'

It wasn't what Chrissie had wanted, it was what she had to do, if she was going to go back to the world and start again.

'Yeah, I suppose so,' said Chrissie. More than anything else she wanted to go back to the world now. She could probably have a proper talk with her mum, now her dad was dead.

The airlock door clanged shut. Chrissie thought that it was a warm sound, it reminded her of the time she heard it when she was in cryo and surfed sleepily on its sound wave. She curled up with her mermaid cushion on the padded rear bulkhead. She felt quite at home and was sure everything was going to be all right.

The Neptunians couldn't wait for entropy to begin. As soon as the airlock shut, without Shorter touching the controls, the main rockets and the boosters came on at the same time, which was forbidden, Shorter would have told them, because it overheated the exhaust deflectors. Punting's whisky jumped from the paper cup and went all over his cravat, as *The Fair Viol* briskly sprang up the tiny ramp and headed for the giant hole above. Shorter felt his eyeballs pushed back into his head. The G-forces were so hard and sharp that for a few seconds Punting could hardly push his tongue out of his mouth to try and suck up the spirit which kept on being dragged horizontally past his face. Pagey was looking down because the gunner had no head rest and he couldn't hold his head up, when he saw all the lights of the city go out together. As they flashed through the giant hole he saw the reason why.

Round the perimeter, set in the rock, were giant electrical substations, in illuminated caves and galleries, with huge cables and girders which indicated a partly buried, perfect circle. The hole was in fact one giant induction ring, a relic of the time when freighters were all as underpowered as the 'Z' series. They hadn't needed to use the ring for hundreds of years, and when they had turned it on for ZV-3, the city's grid had been drained to the last electron in the bid for pain *Xontrol*, by sending the intruders back the way they came.

> *The future will be all right if you fight the good fight,*
> *The future will be fine if you shine that light!*
> *Say one thing for the future, it is out of sight!*
>
> *Don't let's get too parvenue,*
> *Let's reach out for something new*
> *A glittering pile of brand new days*
> *For me*
> *And you!*

When the ringing in his ears had subsided from the takeoff, Shorter tried the controls again to find they were as usual locked. He was annoyed. It was one thing to refit the cabin, and very nice it was too, but poor old ZV-3 didn't have the subframe for 'Safe Among The Stars' type burnoffs like that. But there was no doubt that *they* knew how to place an escape trajectory. Boosted by the spin of the planet, the ship was now already approaching the speed at which they'd arrived. They were pointed back along the path of the planets, which were still lined up like fishing floats, towards 0°.00′.00″ Libra, which provided you didn't think too much about it, made perfect sense, since that was the direction that they'd arrived from. As Neptune slipped away astern, Shorter's head began to clear. Alone of all the surviving crew, he hadn't had any intoxicating substances, but he still had a hard time figuring out what was going on. Pluto's ill-defined mass edged under the nose, without seeming to make any kind of effect on the track of the ship. When it had passed astern Shorter had some trouble even remembering what colour it was. Purplish-brown? Grey-green? Anyhow, it was gone.

Betty told him about her and Chrissie's adventures. Punting had disappeared to the toilet and Shorter moved over so Betty could change back into uniform behind the flying duck screen. In theory, Shorter thought, if you got in the club, you should go with the consequences and have it, and handing it over to the Plutonians was the same as abortion, since they sounded a rough and irresponsible lot. Betty said it was Chrissie's life which was at stake, and at sixteen you'd hardly started to live. Shorter said he was pleased when his wife got pregnant, and he'd feel the same way about his daughter Cynthia, and that was just the way it was. He couldn't see any sense in denying people the right to life. But Betty said there were plenty of people who killed themselves or went into cryo knowing they'd never come back which was the same thing, because life for them was so awful, and she was just trying to help Chrissie along so that she would feel life was worth living, and she wouldn't be able to make a lot of progress in that direction if she went back to Battersea – provided they got back –

on her own with no job and no skills and a little kid.

Shorter said that bringing up kids was Woman's Mission. He'd had quite a hand in bringing up his own but he was a lot more domestic than most men. Betty said that if he thought of himself as different from the norm why couldn't he think of women as verging from the norm without penalty. Shorter said he didn't know, but that was just the way it was with him. He might change, but he found it far more difficult to change his own ideas about women. Giving women the right to kill little things growing in them was like allowing women to declare war at will on the human race. This option of universal belligerence had long been the preserve of men and they were not going to surrender the cherished privilege without a struggle. He warned Betty that she was tampering with deep unconscious feelings beyond her own control if she tried to turn Chrissie into anything more than a Prole mum, or a Cryo.

Betty liked Shorter for the most part except his ferocious prissiness. It was as if there was a little old woman inside him who wouldn't let go. However the deed had been done for Chrissie, so instead of using her insights to devastate or 'shrink-fry' Shorter, Betty kept her own counsel, since it wouldn't help to row, and she looked out of the window and watched Uranus move by. It was yellowish, and rotating bizarrely on its side.

'Pagey's planet,' Shorter observed. 'At any rate that's what he says. It's a very *masculine* planet.'

Pagey came up to join them. His use of drugs had played havoc with his libido over the years. With the exception of the act attempted on Betty which led to the scales falling from Easey's eyes, he hadn't had the urge to do more than poke idly at the worn-out pages of his *Split Beaver Scratch'n'Sniff*, the poor man's Feely. Pagey sniffed his dyeline-stained finger. The old gods of Uranus, Osiris and Ouranos, had been castrated. Pagey reflected it was probably a kinder fate than to be left with a burnt-out desire and a pile of remaindered *S'n'S*, which Mudroche had ruthlessly pushed out of business with the Feely boom.

Shorter had made up his mind long ago on where the frontier to civilised life should be drawn, and no argument was going to change it. As the issue concerned a third party, they were able, as old friends, to let it drop with Pagey's timely entrance. Betty asked him what he had been doing to be wearing a sopping apron in the middle of Millionaire's Park.

'I did all this coke. About a yard of it. Then some speed. Then like a fool I went and did a restaurant.' Shorter smiled pityingly. Betty gasped. 'Fortunately I had so much speed on that I was able to take over from the dishwasher when it broke down after they found I couldn't pay. But they still said that if I dropped below three thousand plates an hour they'd chop my arms off. Then suddenly, they threw me out.'

Pagey was naturally attuned to the gestalt frequency, being entirely paranoid, and had gravitated immediately to the assembly spot. He had known when he wasn't wanted, unlike Punting.

Punting was trimming his moustache in the toilet, which was as good as new, or better, since it had clean soap, towels, and Shorter's own brand of flushing disinfectant which Punting had used to neutralise some of the blood on his shirt. There was a full bottle of cologne, which Punting used to clean himself up with further, and a box of suppositories, he was pleased to notice, since he'd been aware of a burning, itching sensation ever since the Thought police had come down on him. Perhaps it had been the only way in to him for their Thoughts. Punting popped one and the ache from his piles dwindled to nothing. He opened the door in time to catch the fag-end of Pagey's story about going to a restaurant, and he really had a good laugh over that. With a bluff 'Excuse me' he handed Betty her dress, which was lying on his seat (what *were* things coming to?), and settled down to a short nap. His fleshy eyelids went down over his poached-egg eyes at the same time as his eyes rolled up into his head, and he was asleep. Betty went back to give out the call sign. But they were by Saturn and they'd have had to wait hours for a reply even if anyone heard them. In the end, she folded her dress neatly and put it with the new shoes in the parachute locker. She smiled at Chrissie, who was looking drowsy, hanging on to her mermaid cushion at the back. If she was bored, she could do Betty's job for a bit. It wasn't every girl after all who got the chance of trying out a career like that. But when Betty suggested it to her, she said she was quite happy as she was.

Shorter came back to look out of the gunner's window at Neptune, which was now a green fingernail round Pluto's muddy brown. How the colours seemed to alter! He was convinced that the planets weren't this close together normally. *They* had telescoped the radius of the solar system as well as everything else. Shorter looked at Not-Easey, sprawled out on the engineer's toolchest, trying to make sense of his new hands, as if he was a piano player about to begin.

'You sit up the sharp end. You pretend you're driving. But there's still something else taking this ship.'

'Maybe *we've* gone below the event threshold. Here, Easey, what d'you make of that idea?' Not-Easey raised his head slowly and spoke, while his hands writhed out an inaudible sonata.

'Believe me, Neptune is no hallucination. I lived there all my life. The people, the earthquakes, the medical informers, may all be some fantasy to you, but they're my history.' Not-Easey's sluggish watch inched forward another second and his borrowed body suddenly broke wind loudly. Pagey looked up immediately.

'That was *well* over the event threshold.' He stood up and shouted to the sleepy cabin, 'All right!' ''Oo farted then?' Neptunians never lost control of themselves to that extent, and Not-Easey wished that his home planet would quickly take him away. But he had no idea of how they were going to rescue him. The smell had reached Chrissie who had jumped up and was flapping her hands to disperse it. There were districts of Neptune where it was a capital offence. What were they going to do to him?

But Chrissie came and sat next to him, looking friendly. She kicked her heels on the toolbox and looked him straight in the eye.

'That was *you* what cut the cheese, wasn't it?' Not-Easey nodded dumbly, then realised with a slight shiver that the body's previous inhabitant had been in love with Chrissie, and if he wasn't careful he would be seduced into some dreadful tug of war between choosing Neptune and wherever the Earthlings were going to end up when entropy had re-established. He could see the body's point. Chrissie's vitality was growing too, minute by minute, as forceful and direct as her earlier rejection of life. There was more than a hint of the Space-Queen about her, a fire that would never be tied down again in the icy suicide of the state Cryo Programme. Not-Easey had been a woman and had none of Easey's fears about touching people, but still stiffened when Chrissie hugged him. He begged silently for the music of Neptune to take him, before he was trapped for ever by the Earth. There was no doubt that in Chrissie, the old Easey had found his Space Queen, and the new Easey fought in vain against the rising tide of love. He felt his arms move round Chrissie's back, and she laughed as a string of beads came away from the dress into his hand. She plaited it into his hair.

As she did so, he began to hear music. It was as if the space-pearls were somehow picking up a station from Neptune. Actually, it was indeed the music that announced his dissolution, but it was Chrissie's song. It hung about them palpably, as if Easey's fish-white hands had plaited it from the air:

Space Queen!
You with the stars in your dress
Dazzling our eyes
Obscene
Any disguise that hides
Any part of you!
Are you ready?

And Chrissie's hot breath whispered in his ear, that the stars were her father, but her mother was her soul. Not-Easey felt a sudden wrench. He had expected to be rescued in the flesh, but he realised that the ever-subtle shocktroops of the hospitals had more ethereal modes for his consciousness and essence to be lifted back out of negative entropy into a spare body and brain. It was as if his mind was a pan of milk which was being constantly skimmed. Every time it happened, he became less himself, invisibly diminished.

Are you ready?

The stars are my father
But my mother is my soul

Space Queen, he murmured to Chrissie, in a tune only she should hear, you can rock and roll. There was less of him every moment, but her eyes shone back at him in love.

Punting woke up and wanted his lucky fish. He went stumbling about the cabin asking for it. His hands were trembling.

'All right to drive, are you?' Pagey asked him. Punting glared at him.

'That is not the problem.' Punting turned and pointed at Chrissie. 'The problem is *her*. There's our little albatross. But instead of being a dead albatross, hung around some delirious sailor's neck, it's a live one, who has taken us for a ride so that it can smash up its own little eggs.'

Punting now had everybody's attention.

'You brought her on board,' said Pagey quietly.

'It doesn't matter who the agent was who introduced her into this environment. Nothing alters the fact that we all have been cynically manipulated ever since its reappearance from a capsule. We have all been victims of a plot which would involve the suppression of life. And where's it going to end? If she aborts today, then we might be snuffed out tomorrow. She doesn't care for us. She thinks that we're some figment of her malicious imagination. Unless we get rid of her we are never going to escape back into normal entropy. She's the door. If we want to get back, we're going to have to *act*.' Punting's little sleep had been filled with terror, as he dreamed of the gap between what they were doing and what they should have been doing. As he spoke, the rest of the crew became worried too.

'It's simple. We've been bewitched. The witch is there. Instead of carrying and nourishing life, she has been involved in murdering it.'

'So what do you want to do?' Shorter thought old Punting had a point but it seemed a bit hard on Chrissie who had the makings of quite a nice girl if she ever got over her unfortunate family life. In this situation, though, Shorter would never risk going against Punting and would lay the responsibility off on to him. Maybe it *was* all Chrissie's fault. What were the rules in negative entropy? Nobody seemed to know. Chrissie had gone silent as a stone and was clutching at Not-Easey. Punting made a vague effort to pry her off him and put her back in the hold, but she was a big strong girl and soon he stood off to one side huffing like a frustrated bull.

Nobody would help him, or help Chrissie. Mars loomed up, blood-red, but only Betty looked Chrissie in the eye to try and find out how to defuse the situation. It was impossible to know what side Pagey would come down on. But he beckoned her over and said in a low voice that if either of those old *cunts* tried anything on with Chrissie, he'd take the flare pistol and blow them away, and to tell Chrissie, all right?

Betty was as much afraid of a flare pistol fight in the crowded cabin as getting stuck in negative entropy for ever, and she bit her lip nervously, and prayed it wouldn't have to come to either. Punting's sudden upsurge of belligerence began to fade as well. Shorter stayed sitting on the fence, suggesting that they wait till they were up to the point where they had originally experienced the *unusual*, and Chrissie had converted.

'Maybe we won't have to act.' You utter shit, Betty thought, you'd be happy for Chrissie to go back into cryo, if it all happened automatically and you could go back and have your soy-protein shepherd's pie.

Mars slipped behind, its tiny red bulk up against the giant of Jupiter's bulk beyond. Punting sat numbly at the controls, saying nothing, even when the earth in all its beauty slid underneath, side by side with the milky moon. Shorter couldn't see how they could be that close together, since there should be a quarter of a million miles separating them, but then you couldn't know everything about Space. Shorter thought it was like a greenhouse, you never knew exactly why some plants came up and others didn't. It was best to leave the real mysteries to the boys at the *Reader's Digest*. They'd certainly be amused to hear of this one, though it was probably too oddball to make the 'M' issue.

Venus slid by, and in the presence of the planet of love Chrissie hugged Not-Easey again and said whatever happened, thank you for the dress. She then went back to her cushion. Pagey came and sat next to Not-Easey and pushed a flick-knife into one of his large, lifeless hands.

'It's for if that bastard tries anything with Chrissie.' Pagey opened his jacket to show an enormous flare pistol, which would have reduced an elephant to a pile of smoking toenails. Easey put the knife aside. Up front, Punting was crying quietly for the loss of his lucky fish.

'I'm afraid I won't be with you for much longer. I'm being pulled out of this body, back to where I came from.' Pagey looked round wildly for the ropes and tackle which should be doing the job of separating Easey out, but there was nothing to be seen.

'This is goodbye. I'm leaving through the nose.'

'Will we get the old Easey back?' Pagey was hot for allies.

'I've no idea.' Not-Easey slipped then recovered his balance on the toolbox. 'Sorry. I'm going very fast.' This sounded to Pagey like running away.

'Can't you hold your nose and stop it coming out?' Not-Easey's eyes looked at him sadly, saying, don't make me stay. But Pagey grabbed hold of his nose for him, and Not-Easey's new arms felt unfamiliar and weak.

'What the fuck has been going on here?'

'Led go an I tell you.'

'If I let go you'll piss off, you said!'

Easey slowly pushed Pagey's grip aside. He said faintly, 'I wouldn't worry if I were you. You're going to be all right.'

'What, we're going to go back to what it was before?'

Not-Easey nodded.

'What about the rest of them?'

'They'll be all right.'

'What's all right? Is Chrissie going to be all right?' Pagey had been in this position too many times before. The vague promises, the dark street, the shifty dealer. He grabbed hold of Not-Easey's nose again.

'She'll get what she originally wanted.'

It was as Pagey had suspected. They were going to round it all off by putting her back into cryo. No mess, no loose ends.

'She doesn't want what she originally wanted, sonny. You know that. Now not so fast through those adenoids. Either you arrange for her to stay out or I'm going to hang on to your nose till we're back out the other side and half of you is going to be stuck inside Easey for *life*.'

Pagey was at the edge of his bluff, and had no idea what the reply would be. But after a second or so, Not-Easey nodded. Pagey sighed with relief and let go of his nose. Immediately Not-Easey said,

'In that case we will need a substitute.' His eyes looked straight at Pagey, daring him to volunteer for cryo. But Pagey saw the trap. He clapped Not-Easey on the shoulder and stood up.

'Captain Punting, a question here from Easey which he wanted me to ask you. When the time comes, would you yourself choose to be cryogenically frozen?' This was one of ten standard questions to which the cryo captains had to learn the answer off by heart, for the instruction of novice journalists.

Punting turned round with lowered lids and gave the required answer.

'As captain of one of Her Majesty's Freighters, I can confidently recommend the ride to *anyone*.' Easey nodded. The substitute, using only the words required by the publicity department of the Ministry of Space, had effectively volunteered. Praise be to our guardians, who shall tell us what we should say!

Shorter came back suspiciously to where Pagey stood to find out what was going on. They were closing fast to the position. Pagey whispered for him not to go back, because he'd made a deal, so that on re-entry Punting, not Chrissie, would convert. Shorter was appalled at the thought.

'You made a deal? What kind of a deal?'

'With Easey.'

'What kind of negotiating powers has Easey got in this situation?' Pagey was a stranger to union talk.

'He said he could fix it.'

'Were you dealing with the top management? Do you know if he knows what it's all about?'

'It's not your kind of negotiation, Shorter, it's street dealing. It's the only kind I know.'

Not-Easey's nose twitched as if he was going to sneeze. Pagey watched it closely. Where's my lucky fish, Punting moaned, where's my lucky fish?

'What do you mean, Easey promised you all that? He's an *idiot*. He's not *anybody*.'

They both looked at Not-Easey. He solemnly reached up to blow his nose, on his sleeve it seemed. But a grey-green plasma started ballooning out of his nostrils, joined by little trickles from his eyes, and his arm fell listlessly down to his side. Pagey smiled. The plasma swelled, burst and was gone, leaving nothing. Not-Easey was gone from Easey's body.

'Well, whoever it was, we can't find out now.'

Chrissie was oblivious to all the dealing on her behalf. She knew it wasn't her fault what had happened, it was because of her desires that they had got dragged into some sideways universe, but she feared the prophetic dreams of cryo and its stillness, in her present mood it would be all pain. She prayed to the Ministry of Space, promising them any amount of babies, later, if they would only now intervene cosmically and put her back on the wheel. Shorter stood his distance from her, in case she was going to convert there and then. She felt like a leper. Even Betty had forgotten about her and was afraid for herself, it looked like.

In fact, Betty was experiencing the dizziness which preceded their last transfer. She had stomach cramps. Shorter made as if to go back to the controls but fell on the floor as the zebra patterns cartwheeled and swirled around. Then, there was a kind of squeaky pop, and they were *through*.

The Scorpion, Scales, Ram, Archer, Lion and Virgin swung round obligingly to their old positions in the zodiac, as did the Crab, the Bull, the Fishes, the Twins, the Water Bearer and the Goat. Shorter, struggling with his vertigo, pushed his way past the curtain with the flying ducks, and slammed himself down in front of the controls. As far as he could gather from a quick look, the solar system had rearranged itself as they had left it, and they had come back close to the earth. The engines were off and they were in high orbit, in the dropping zone in fact.

The controls felt good. Using the steering jets, Shorter manoeuvred them past a cryo cargo which had been dumped in space God knows how many years ago. It was tumbling, slowly, end over end, accompanied by a little cloud of silver bottles. There was a starburst at the side. Sometimes the orbiting Cryos were used for target practice for death rays or hunter/killer satellites, you saw a lot of it if you flew the Cryo. It was disgraceful, of course, but what could you do? It was no worse than boys digging up Highgate cemetery to play with the corpses. In the end, you could get used to anything.

There was a loud clicking in Punting's seat next to him. Shorter glanced down and saw that there was a canister lying there. He yelled for Pagey, who came and lifted it up in his dirty white rayon scarf, and took it away. There was a crash as he threw it in the hold and shut the hatch. The street deal had worked. Punting had gone.

Betty even managed to raise Gatwick, who told them to go to a lower dropping orbit, as they were in one which was full. Shorter knew that the lower orbits could often be moved around by pressure from the solar wind and could often be tripped into orbits which were going to be air-frictive one day. And then the whole lot would burn up. He would drop it there, but only under protest. Apart from the laconic instruction, ground control were totally uninterested in where they'd been, and after a question about the time, started relaying the nine o'clock news instead of answering questions. What was strange was that all the Neptunian spit and polish seemed to have gone for nothing in the re-entry, and instead of a gleaming chariot he was left piloting the old ZV-3 pumpkin with a cracked pilot's window and star maps slowly turning to lint. Still, there was a certain sense of achievement, he couldn't exactly pin it down in words, about seeing the stars in their courses again. If ground control didn't come in again he'd go manual on the dropping orbit shortly: there was really no point in putting it where they said and he wasn't going to comply if they weren't going to work with him.

There was just enough fuel left for a re-entry orbit. Shorter licked the fluff off his pencil and began calculations that would allow a minimum of stress on that dodgy window. It would have to be a slow descent. As for Punting, there was no harm in leaving reporting that till they got to the ground. He couldn't see how they could have acted otherwise. If they wanted him, they could come and get him, before he burned.

Pagey smiled triumphantly at Betty and Chrissie as he came back in. But Chrissie was holding Not-Not-Easey and Betty was listening to the news. The Xontroller of the Cryogenic Programme, a bloke named Carwash, had been found wrecking a cryo plant. He had done several million pounds' worth of damage. Naturally, they were going to torch him.

'Here, d'you realise that one of his last acts would have been to pass princess here? Except he told her not to go or something.' But Chrissie was trying to wake Not-Not-Easey up by gently shaking him, and hadn't heard. The rest of the news was about the Russian scare, but Betty turned it off, feeling suddenly sorry for Carwash, who she'd never met. What on earth had possessed him to do a thing like that?

Pagey picked his gum off the breech of the gun and started scanning the skies restlessly for cheeky MIG 240s. *The Fair Viol*'s orbit moved into the earth's shadow and a brief night.

Chrissie was shaking Not-Not-Easey violently now, and moaning, saying, Easey! Easey! But his eyes had gone up to the top of his head, like Punting's when he prepared for sleep, though his eyelids were still open.

'Careful now! Or his head'll come off,' said Pagey wittily. Shorter told Betty to inform Gatwick that they had lined up for the drop. Betty, not expecting any reply, had given the call sign and then said, can you clear us to relict cargo orbit? There was no reply so she just left the key in with the volume turned up, so they could hear if Gatwick said anything. Chrissie was now making a terrible noise. Betty was all for having a nice cry but this was ridiculous. Pagey stood up and went over to her where she was hitting and slapping Not-Not-Easey, and lying on top of him as if he had sunstroke and she was Elijah. None of them could hardly think, with the noise she made.

Pagey was quite rough with her because there was so little time to go to the drop. He told her that none of them knew him, even less her, and if she didn't pull herself together and stop making that noise she'd find herself back in the hold. This didn't make any difference either, to her.

'Look, Chrissie, don't mind him. What about me? I did a deal. *I* saved your life. Understand? Now be grateful.'

Chrissie stared up at him, uncomprehendingly. Pagey mistook the silence for submission.

'I'll take you out tonight an' all,' he added kindly.

Chrissie gazed down at the senseless body in her arms, and then up at the man who had offered to take her out tonight, and past him at the other heartless zombies, flicking their switches.

'What has made you all so *cruel?*' she said, finally. There was a long silence. Shorter felt she was a fine one to talk, but there was no time for anything but the job in hand. Pagey took over the engineer's drop-handle, which looked more like a giant cheese-cutter than anything. He had to push Chrissie off the box to get to it and now she was wallowing in all the dirt which had mysteriously returned to the ship as if it had never been away. He shouted he was standing by to drop.

Chrissie watched through the veil of her tears as her first true love lay inert in her arms. She was numb with grief and it was almost a relief in a way when the crew began a numeric panto- mime, Shorter and Pagey shouting a countdown slowly to each other. Chrissie didn't care if they were counting down to the last trump. The activity stopped the ache in her brain.

Ten! shouted Shorter and Pagey one after another. Nine! Eight! They were absurd, like a couple of crazy truck-drivers she had once met in a caff, who used to do the same kind of act. By the time they had got to the drop and visual confrontation of cargo away, as the freighter detached itself with a big clunk, she had almost forgotten what it was they were doing.

They edged away from orbit and the silver cargohold drifted up and out of sight. Betty's radio link was still open, waiting for Gatwick, and for a few moments they all listened to the interfer- ence. There was the customary chatter of short-wave, and then the trilling of hydrogen clouds deep in other galaxies, not unlike the noise the starlings make when they gather at dusk in Leicester Square.

Chrissie took counsel with her womb and found it to be empty, as empty as Easey's head. It had begun to be cold in ZV-3, round the dark side, but it got warm again as Shorter started cautiously on the long, slow, re-entry.